Chowder

A Hooked and Cooked Cozy Mystery Series

by Lyndsey Cole

Connect with me:

Lyndsey@LyndseyColeBooks.com

www.facebook.com/LyndseyColeAuthor

Chapter 1

Rustic, she wrote.

Cozy, she insisted. Or was the exact word *charming*?

You'll love living on the beach.

No exaggeration with that statement. Hannah Holiday couldn't wait to leave the congestion of California. It certainly had its own crazy charm, but who wouldn't choose to live on the beach over just about anywhere else? Many nights she imagined the salty ocean smell and the rhythmic crashing of waves lulling her to sleep. Now, she would smell and hear the real deal.

Hannah stood with her back to the crashing surf, hands on her hips, and surveyed the rundown, weathered cottages. Her Great Aunt Caroline sure did dump a mess in Hannah's lap. And there wasn't much she could do about it. No giving it back.

The contents of Caroline's will were spelled out with every *t* crossed and every *i* dotted. Hannah couldn't sell for at least one year. Caroline left enough money and more to pay the taxes and at least get started with renovations.

She was a shrewd one, that Great Aunt Caroline. She'd always wanted Hannah to help her with her business, and now with her death, Caroline figured out how to make it happen.

The front of the café, which wasn't much more than a snack bar, was boarded up with plywood and the sign, *Caroline's Café & Cottages*, hung precariously from one nail.

"You the new owner?"

Hannah spun around, her long braid swinging over her shoulder. "You startled me."

"Hope you're not planning on tearing the place down." A man, not much taller than

Hannah, stared at her with eyes the color of the ocean. "You're not one of those big fancy city developers, are you?" His eyes slowly traveled from the top of her windblown hair to the flip flops on her feet. "No, I reckon not." He pointed to her feet. "I hope you packed some warm socks in that backpack. It's not even close to being summer here."

Hannah bristled. Who was this guy asking her questions and telling her how to dress? For all she knew, he could be homeless and he was probably worried about losing squatters rights in one of the four cabins she was the reluctant new owner of. "And you are?" She puffed herself up, trying to look bigger than her five and a half foot, one hundred thirty pound self.

"Alton Jackson the Third," he threw his shoulders back, "but folks around here call me Jack. I guess you can call me Jack, too." His eyes squinted as he took a closer look at Hannah. "Caroline told me she had a great niece. Is that you?"

"You knew Great Aunt Caroline?" Hannah's voice softened slightly.

"Sure did. Everyone in these parts knew her. And loved her, too. Or, at least, they loved her cafe. No one did up clam chowder the way Caroline did." Jack gazed off into the distance and licked his lips. He must have been remembering the taste of something delicious. "She had a secret ingredient. I hope she left you her recipes along with this run-down mess."

A loud crash made Hannah jump clear off the ground.

Jack chuckled a deep throaty, almost growling laugh. "Better get used to stuff falling down around here. That sign won't be the last crash you hear unless you get busy right quick." His eyes narrowed. "You're not going to level these cottages, are you?"

"I can't. Caroline left all this beauty to me with the condition that the only changes I make are to remodel, refurbish, and reroof what's already here. Her exact wording." Hannah swept her arms wide, indicating the four, one and two room cottages, and the tiny café.

Another chuckle emerged from deep inside Jack's chest. "Sounds just like what she'd do. All those fancy types that showed up never managed to entice her even with the offer of millions for this spot. She didn't care much about money. Yup, once she knew what they were after, she wouldn't even sell them a bowl of clam chowder." He laughed. "She ran a few of 'em off with her shotgun. I don't think she had a clue how to even load the darn thing but they could never be sure what she might do." He pointed his gnarled finger at Hannah. "You best keep that shotgun handy, young lady."

"Shotgun?" Hannah flinched at the thought of touching a gun.

"It doesn't matter if you know how to use it but there's one persistent fella that was comin' round regular as clockwork. The owner of the Paradise Inn—Vern Mason. I haven't seen him since just before your Great Aunt Caroline died, but you'll know him by his polo shirt. He always wears a bright blue polo shirt, ocean blue he always said, khaki pants, and a black leather belt with an odd buckle. Looks like a wave. Said it made him look like he fit in but he stood out like a big fat swollen thumb with that New York accent of his."

"You were good friends with Great Aunt Caroline?" Hannah asked, realizing she knew no one in Hooks Harbor now that Caroline was dead. Jack wasn't exactly her type, more like the complete opposite—gruff and at least fifty years her senior with no tact whatsoever—but maybe he could introduce her to some locals. May was only five months away and she would need a lot of help to get the cottages ready to rent before the busy season started.

Jack's eyes filled and he blinked several times. "Yes, you could say that. She was a special girl."

Girl? Hannah never thought of her eighty three year old great aunt as a girl, but Jack appeared to be from that decade, too. It was all relative in the eyes of the beholder.

"Now, take some advice from me. What's your name?"

"Hannah."

"Hannah," he said, more to himself, working the name through his memory bank. "Caroline did mention you. A lot. What took you so long to get yourself out here? You should have come to help before Caroline died. Would have made it a lot easier on you, ya know. And her for that matter."

Hannah sighed and wiped a tear from her cheek. "I can't go back and do it over now, can I? What's the advice you were going to give me?"

He pointed to a small, tidy, grey-shingled house, barely visible down the road. "That's my place. You come over anytime you need something. Any time of day or night. Don't be bashful."

Hannah's head bobbed up and down and she smiled. "I'll do that."

"Okay then. Fix up that cottage for yourself." He pointed to the biggest one sitting closest to the beach. "That's the one Caroline lived in and there's room enough for a single girl like you and an office space. And get a dog. You might not need that shotgun if you have a dog."

"A dog?"

"As a matter of fact, I have a beauty that would be perfect for you. Are you hungry?"

Hannah's head spun trying to keep up with Jack's jumbled conversation. The idea of tackling all the work to get the cottages and café up and running, adopting a dog, meeting the locals—where to start? And was she even ready for the challenge? "Breakfast sounds perfect." She shouldered her backpack on and waited for Jack to lead the way.

"I didn't say anything about breakfast."

Hannah felt heat rise up her neck and spread over her pale cheeks.

Jack laughed a deep belly laugh. "Well, okay. Nellie will be happy for some company."

"I don't want to intrude," Hannah said with her hands up. "I can get myself some food in town."

"Don't be silly. The company will do us good. And between you and me," he paused and lowered his voice, "the food at the Shipwreck Diner is hit or miss." He turned toward his house and waved his hand, indicating she should follow. "Come on."

Hannah jogged to catch up, her backpack over one shoulder, bouncing against her side. Jack's house was surrounded by a white picket fence with the dried remains of hydrangea blooms against the grey weathered shingles of his house.

He opened the front door, holding it so Hannah could enter first. A wiggly puppy darted across the room, launching herself at Hannah's legs.

Jack laughed. "Slow down Nellie, you'll scare the poor girl away."

Hannah, crouched at Nellie's level, tilted her head back to look up at Jack. "This is Nellie?"

"Yeah, who were you expecting?"

"Oh. I thought Nellie was someone you lived with."

Jack hung his jacket on the hook next to the door. "Nope. Just me and Nellie at the moment. It appears she's taken a liking to you. She'll be good company over at your new cottage. You take her out for a walk while I get the food cooking. You like omelets?"

Hannah was wondering what she was walking into but, whatever, it was time to go with the flow and get out of her comfort zone. "Omelet? Sure, sounds delicious. Do you need help?"

"Yup. Help with Nellie. Her leash is hanging next to the door. Now, take her outside before she pees all over the floor."

Without another word, Jack walked into his kitchen just beyond the small living room Hannah stood in. She opened the door, letting Nellie run outside. Hannah watched the golden blur zoom around the yard, leaping and twisting in obvious delight at the freedom. Hannah attached the leash, opened the gate, and they headed up the street. In the opposite direction of her new home.

Hannah guessed Nellie's age to be about four or five months. She was beyond the new puppy stage but was still a clumsy, uncoordinated teen with way too big feet. Nellie ran to the end of her leash toward a man walking on the opposite side of the road. He was completely engrossed in a conversation on his phone.

"I said I'd be there in a half hour," Hannah overheard the man say just before he tripped and his phone flew from his hand. A string of curses followed.

Hannah quickened her pace trying to avoid any potential interaction with his anger. She and Nellie took a right turn down a quiet road with several small homes, then two more rights, ending up back on Ocean View Lane between Jack's house and her newly inherited project.

Hannah heard the shriek of a smoke alarm when she got to Jack's front door. The scent of burnt toast accosted her nose.

"Are you okay?" she yelled on her way to the kitchen.

Jack pulled the batteries from the alarm, silencing the deafening screech.

"Breakfast is ready," he announced, ignoring her question as if this was a normal occurrence.

Two places were set at the small, round kitchen table. Mismatched plates held a mess of what was supposed to be an omelet with triangles of black toast on either side.

Hannah sat in the chair by the wall. A steaming mug of coffee sat in front of her plate.

Jack sat across from her. "Dig in before everything gets cold. It tastes better than it looks."

Hannah waited for Jack to ask her about her walk but he dug into his food as if he hadn't eaten for days.

Tentatively, Hannah sipped her coffee, hoping it hadn't met the same fate as the toast. It was perfect. Rich, dark and strong.

Just how she liked it. With the caffeine surging through her veins, she ate a forkful of the eggs. A smile spread across her face. "Delicious."

"Yup. I have three hens out back. Nothing like homegrown eggs."

They ate in silence until all the food was gone. Every last crumb. Even the burnt toast.

Jack leaned back in his chair, holding his coffee. A burp escaped through his lips. "Sorry, I'm not used to having company."

Hannah felt her lip twitch. "Thanks for the food. Just what I need before I tackle the day."

"There's a friend of mine I'd like you to meet. Cal Murphy. You'll like him, and he could help you with the fixing up you need to do."

Hannah hemmed and hawed, not sure that any friend of Jack's would be young enough to be of much help, and how did he know who she would like? “I’ll let you know when I’m ready for that.” She pushed her chair back and brought her plate and mug to the sink. “Thanks Jack. I’ll get out of your way.”

“Don’t be shy about stopping by. And don’t forget to take Nellie. She’s too much for an old man like me.”

Nellie followed Hannah to the sink, dancing around her feet.

“Yup, she wants to go with you. Don’t worry, I’ll come visit and bring you some nice brown homegrown eggs, too,” Jack said.

Hannah patted Nellie. Her fur was as soft as silk. She would be good company. “Okay, I’ll take her on a trial basis.” It all felt too weird to Hannah. Who dumped a dog on someone they barely knew?

Jack stood at the sink washing the dishes, his back to Hannah. His deep chuckle was his only response.

Hannah shook her head, feeling a bit awkward as she snapped the leash on Nellie's collar and let herself outside. The day was promising to be one of those December gifts. Brilliant blue sky, a few puffy clouds, and a slight ocean breeze carrying the smell of salt and the sound of gulls. Hannah breathed deeply, savoring the moment until her arm was yanked by Nellie running down the street, pulling Hannah toward their new home and a couple of visitors.

As Hannah approached the sandy entrance to her café and cottages, she could hear loud arguing. Great, she wondered, who is quarreling on my doorstep?

Nellie barked and lunged, drawing the attention of two men. They stared at Hannah and she stared back. One man wore a blue polo shirt under a thick sweatshirt, and the other, a bit younger, leaner, and more weathered, wore jeans and a denim jacket.

“Who are you?” the stouter man asked.

“I’m not sure it’s any of your business. You’re trespassing. Please leave. Now.” She slid her cell phone from her jean pocket, not even sure who she would call but hoping it would bluff these two to leave.

“Trespassing? You’re the owner?” the second man asked.

Hannah stared, saying nothing.

The weathered man extended his hand, approaching Hannah, “I’m Chase Fuller, owner of Bayside Marina.”

Hannah recognized him as the man talking on his phone that she saw earlier while walking Nellie.

The other man elbowed Chase out of the way, “I’m Vern Mason. I was a good friend of the previous owner, Caroline Holiday.”

"Really," Hannah said as a statement with her eyebrows raised. "Funny that my great aunt never mentioned you."

Vern's face turned bright red. He blustered, "Well, business acquaintances. You know what I mean. I own the Paradise Inn and Caroline owned these charming seaside cottages. As a matter of fact, I had a contract to buy this whole place but she died before it was finalized. I guess I'll be dealing with you now." He smiled but Hannah could see it was one of those sleazy salesman forced smiles.

She walked past the two men, punching a number into her phone with Nellie sticking close to her legs. She opened the door of the main cottage, not sure what she would do next until her eyes fixated on Caroline's shotgun resting against the wall. Hannah picked up the gun, being careful to keep it pointed away from anyone in case it decided to explode. She walked back outside, and with a firm, serious voice told Vern and Chase, "I asked you to leave."

They looked at each other, then at Hannah before walking back out the way they must have come in.

As she leaned the gun next to the door, she overheard Chase say to Vern, "Just like her crazy aunt, but I won't let you steal that property out from under me. Again."

Chapter 2

A loud crack brought Hannah upright in her bed. Was she dreaming? Was it a door slamming shut somewhere? Nellie barked and ran to the cottage door. Hannah pulled her jeans on as she hopped across the cold floor. She grabbed her flip flops, forgetting they would be useless against the cold outside. At least her warm jacket was hanging on a hook next to the door and she pulled it on.

Only a few gulls broke the silence when she peered outside. With no clue what she heard, she ventured a few steps onto the sandy path, searching left and right for a hint as to what made the noise. Nellie bolted over the rocks toward the beach and the ocean.

Great, Hannah thought. She increased her speed, hoping not to lose sight of the puppy. She didn't bother putting her flip flops on so she could run faster and, hopefully, catch Nellie before the silly puppy ran all the way to the next town.

Nellie jumped up on a figure walking toward Hannah. At least she could slow down and catch her breath.

"What are you doing out here, Nellie?" the man said as he crouched down while Nellie gave his face a bath.

Hannah's shadow fell on the man and he looked up into her face. "You must be Jack's new neighbor. He told me someone moved in." He held his hand out toward Hannah. "I'm Cal. Cal Murphy."

Hannah shook his hand, noticing how rough and strong it was. As he stood up, she looked into his face. Handsome in a rugged sort of way. His face was tan even for December. An outdoorsy guy? Hannah guessed he was a bit older than her twenty seven years but not anywhere close to Jack's age. He brushed his sandy blond hair out of his blue eyes and they appeared to twinkle with the sunshine.

He smiled with one eyebrow raised. “And you are?” he prompted Hannah.

She blinked a couple of times. “Sorry. Hannah Holiday.”

Another couple of booms caused Hannah to startle.

Cal laughed. “That’s just some blasting for the new bridge.”

Hannah nodded her head. “It woke us up. I had no idea what it was. For all I knew, it could have been the two men who showed up on my doorstep yesterday shooting each other.”

“You must be talking about Vern and Chase. Those two would turn a beautiful day like this into an argument.” Cal glanced at her bare feet and the edges of his lips curled up slightly. “I’m heading to Jack’s house. He’ll have a strong pot of coffee ready if you need some." He tilted his head, waiting for a reply.

Hannah slipped her flip flops on. "That sounds great." She matched his gait and Nellie lead the way straight to Jack's house.

Cal opened the door without knocking, waiting for Nellie and Hannah to enter first. "Jack, you need to set out a couple more mugs for coffee."

Hannah loved the smell of coffee, and after being treated to Jack's brew the day before, her brain anticipated the jolt.

"Just who I was expecting. Come on in and make yourselves comfortable," Jack said as he took the lid off a cookie jar and tossed a treat to Nellie. He set a bowl of water on the floor for her and she lapped it up, dripping on the linoleum when she was done.

"Today's a good day to show Hannah around town. No point in waiting for everyone to drop by out of curiosity."

Hannah sipped the hot dark liquid. "I met a couple of locals yesterday when I got home."

Jack raised an eyebrow. "Let me guess. Chase and Vern?"

"How did you know?"

"They're just like a couple of vultures when it comes to Caroline's property. Did you have the shotgun ready?"

Cal choked and his coffee spilled over the side of his cup. "Shotgun? I'm glad I didn't show up bright and early on your doorstep this morning."

Hannah laughed. "Yes, as a matter of fact. It was ready and waiting right inside, and when I walked out holding the gun, they both took off, mumbling something about me being crazy just like my aunt."

"Be careful you don't shoot yourself in the foot with that thing," Jack warned.

Hannah's mouth dropped open. "I hope Caroline didn't leave it loaded."

Cal chuckled. "It wouldn't surprise me if she did. I'll take a look at it if you want. I can teach you a little bit about guns."

Jack stood up. "Finish up, I told Pam we'd swing by her place first. She's been having some problems with her son again."

Hannah listened to the conversation, hoping either Jack or Cal would fill in the blanks about who these people were. She was going to have to take notes to keep everyone straight. Cal picked up Hannah's mug, carried it to the sink, and rinsed both.

"Who's Pam?" she finally asked.

"She's my daughter and one of the police officers in town. Come on." Jack checked the time. "We've got a few minutes to show Cal what needs to be done to get your café and cottages up and running before we head to Pam's house." He looked at Nellie sprawled on the kitchen floor. "As soon as I open the door, she'll be up and ready to go. Watch."

Jack put his I-heart-Hooks Harbor cap on, picked up his walking stick, and opened the front door. Nellie lifted her head, jumped up, and slid on the slick linoleum trying to get a grip on her way to the front door. They all laughed at the clumsy pup but she managed to catch herself on the rug and she zoomed out the door without a care in the world.

"Where did Nellie come from?" Hannah asked.

"I found her on the beach." He crunched up his lips, thinking. "Maybe two or three weeks ago. She was a mess. Dirty, skinny, and scared of her own shadow. Now she's ready to move in with someone younger than I am. Someone who can keep up with all that energy." With that comment, he headed toward Hannah's new acquisition and she had to jog to keep up, wondering who he was fooling about his energy levels.

They stopped outside the main cottage, where Hannah had spent the previous night. Cal took his cap off and ran his fingers through his hair. "Where do you want to start?"

Hannah started to answer, but Jack interrupted. "She should fix the café first. Get an income stream coming in."

Hannah frowned. "Wait a minute." She opened the door of the cottage. "I want to be comfortable first. This is where *I* want to start."

Cal elbowed Jack. "I guess *she* told you."

The cottage wasn't in too bad shape. Mostly it needed a good cleaning, but Cal made suggestions about what he thought should be upgraded. "This galley kitchen is outdated. How about new counters and appliances?" He opened the bathroom door. "Same here. It's all workable the way it is but if you want an upgrade, now's the time to do it." He took some measurements and made some notes in his notebook. "The floors are in good shape, nothing sanding and new polyurethane wouldn't spruce up. I should check the roof and see about new shingles."

Hannah nodded. Jack frowned. "Why waste your money replacing perfectly functional stuff?" he asked.

Hannah glared but turned her attention to Cal. "Yes. To all of it. Great Aunt Caroline left enough money for me to fix these cottages up and I want to bring them into the twenty first century."

Jack threw his hands up in the air. "Come on Nellie, we'll wait outside. I know when I'm outnumbered."

Cal's lip twitched and a soft chuckle escaped. "Jack likes things to go his way. I think he's met his match."

With Jack out of earshot, Hannah asked Cal about Pam. "His daughter is a police officer?"

"Yup. A good one, too. She doesn't take crap from anyone. Except her son, from what Jack tells me."

"Her son?"

"Yeah, Noah, he's eighteen or nineteen and hangs out with a bad crowd. He's a nice enough kid when he's away from his friends, but he's headed for trouble if he doesn't watch out. And Pam won't be able to protect him from everything if he's not careful."

"I saw a couple of kids walking on the beach last night. I thought they were headed up here to the cottages, but when they saw me and heard Nellie bark, they ran off."

Cal nodded. "Probably Noah and his girlfriend. These cottages were quite the party hangout after your aunt died and no one was living here. You'll have to watch out until they get the message this isn't empty anymore. Do you want me to look at the rest of the buildings now?"

"Might as well if you have time."

Cal smiled. "All the time in the world. It's slow this time of year so I'll be able to get right on your projects. And we've been lucky with the mild weather this December."

When they went outside, Jack's lean figure was just visible down the beach with Nellie darting at the waves before running away from the rushing water. She barked and bit at the foam. Hannah couldn't help but laugh at the antics.

Cal examined the café next. He removed the plywood covering the snack bar area. "This only needs a few new boards and a couple coats of paint. Let's take a look at the inside." He pulled on the door leading to the small space behind the snack bar. The bottom hinge broke, leaving the door hanging lopsided.

Cal tipped his head. “I think a new door will fix this problem.” Inside, everything looked ready for a new season. There were a half dozen tables with a view of the ocean and a small kitchen in the back. “A good scrub and you should be good to go. What next?”

Hannah pointed to the cottages in the back. “I haven’t been inside any of them yet but the last one looks to be in the worst shape.”

Jack was almost back to the cottages by the time Cal opened the door to cottage number four.

Hannah gasped and covered her mouth with her hand. “That’s one of the men who was here yesterday.”

Cal rushed inside to check for a pulse even though by the looks of him, there was no life left in the crumpled body. A big splotch of red stained the blue polo shirt.

Chapter 3

Jack was on the phone.

Cal guided Hannah away from the scene to a picnic table next to the café.

"He was here yesterday," she repeated. "Alive." She sat with her legs splayed in front while leaning back against the table. The waves continued to wash in and out, the sun beat down, warming her head, but she couldn't get rid of the image of the blood soaked polo shirt.

"Looks like Vern finally pushed the wrong person's buttons."

Hannah looked at Cal, her eyes wide. "All because he wanted this piece of property?"

"He did want this property but there are plenty of other reasons someone might want him dead. Pam will sort it all out. I hear the siren now."

Hannah stood up, watching several police cars screech into her quiet spot. An ambulance followed. Too late for them to help, she thought. Jack motioned for a police woman to follow him to cottage number four.

"What's going to happen now?" Hannah asked Cal.

He shrugged. "I suppose we'll have to answer questions before we can leave. This is a crime scene. Do you have someplace else you can stay?"

"I'll figure something out." She didn't have a clue what that something might be but her natural curiosity flipped on, making her determined to find out what happened in cottage number four. Her cottage. Her responsibility.

Jack and the police woman approached Hannah and Cal. Jack introduced Hannah to his daughter, Officer Pam Larson.

Hannah stared at the shotgun Officer Larson was holding, wondering where she found it.

"Is this your gun, Ms. Holiday?"

"Well, it was my Great Aunt Caroline's gun. I guess it's mine now." Hannah thought it was an odd question. They should be gathering evidence and figuring out who murdered Vern instead of asking her about an old gun.

"Did you leave it inside the cottage where we found Vern Mason?"

Hannah's head swiveled to look at the front of her cottage, cottage number one. She knew she left it leaning against the cottage after Vern and Chase left. Or did she bring it inside? "No," she finally answered. "I left it over there." She pointed to her cottage.

"Did you know the victim, Ms. Holiday?"

"No. Yes. I didn't know him. He came here yesterday and introduced himself. Chase somebody or other was with him, too, and they were arguing." Hannah felt Officer Larson's eyes boring into her own. She looked away. What was happening?

"You'll have to come to the police station and give a statement. I'm keeping the gun as evidence."

"Evidence?" Hannah said, her voice barely a whisper.

Officer Pam Larson turned around, heading back to cottage number four. The covered body was wheeled out on a stretcher and the ambulance drove off. Silently.

She looked at Cal. "Does she think I shot Vern?"

Hannah felt his hand on her shoulder. The warmth seeped through her jacket. "Don't worry. This will all get sorted out."

"Sorted out?" Hannah slumped back onto the picnic table bench, all strength drained from her legs.

"Do you want me to take you to the police station?" Cal asked.

Hannah nodded. "I don't even know where it is."

Officer Larson returned, asking Hannah to follow her. Jack said he would keep an eye on Nellie. The drive to the police station was only about ten minutes but it sped by much too quickly for Hannah's liking.

Cal tried to calm her nerves. "Pam is a fair person. Just tell her what you know. She needs to gather all the facts, and Vern *was* found on your property so it makes sense that she's starting with you."

Hannah nodded. She breathed in and out. Slowly. Letting the air work some magic to calm her fears. What did Great Aunt Caroline dump her into? Hannah's mother had always warned her, don't let Caroline suck you into her renegade life as an unmarried business woman. And not even a proper business in their mind, but what they called Caroline's hippy snack shack and beach cottage rental business.

Cal pulled into a parking lot, breaking her from her memories. "I'll go in with you."

Hannah nodded.

The police station was a one story brick building, cold and sterile. It had none of the charm of the downtown buildings with their windows decorated for the Christmas season. A flag snapped in the wind, making Hannah jump.

Cal put his hand on her shoulder. "You don't have anything to be worrying about, do you?"

"Right now? Maybe my future?"

"Just tell Pam what you know. She's after the facts. Don't let her blunt demeanor intimidate you. It's how she is."

"You keep telling me to tell her what I know. I arrived in Hooks Harbor yesterday.

I don't know anything!" Hannah's voice raised to a near panic.

Cal explained at the front desk why they were there and Hannah was guided to an office in the back. Hannah stood in the doorway, waiting for Pam to give her instructions. Pam continued to type on her laptop without acknowledging Hannah's presence.

Finally, she closed her computer and motioned for Hannah to sit in the only chair available. A wooden chair with a straight back. Pam rested her elbows on her desk and entwined her fingers, leaning slightly toward Hannah.

"So, tell me, Ms. Holiday, when did you arrive here in Hooks Harbor?"

"Yesterday morning." Hannah forced herself to answer the question. Only the question. Without any unnecessary chatter even though with her nerves about to explode, her mouth threatened to babble.

"Walk me through your day."

Hannah slowly and carefully tried to remember every detail. She started with meeting Jack, going to breakfast at his house, walking Nellie and seeing the man she thought was Chase walking toward her property. She told Pam about meeting Vern and Chase and how she heard Chase tell Vern he wouldn't let Vern steal the property from him again.

Pam sat up straighter. "Do you remember the exact words?"

Hannah looked around the office. "Yes, he said, 'just like her crazy aunt, but I won't let you steal that property out from under me. Again.' He was so angry, it sent chills up my spine when he said it."

"Did you threaten them to leave?"

Hannah felt a rush of heat in her cheeks. "I was scared. I saw my great aunt's gun leaning just inside the front door of her cottage. Well, it's mine now." She stared at

Pam. "I didn't even think about what I was doing, but I picked up the gun and walked back outside. I didn't point it at them or anything. I just walked back outside and asked them to leave. That's when I heard Chase's words to Vern."

"What time did all this happen?"

"I think it was late morning. I don't know the exact time. After they left, I took Nellie for a walk on the beach to think about my next step with the café and cottages." She paused. "I was trying to sort out if I was up for the task."

"Did you figure it out?" Pam offered her first somewhat friendly smile but it looked forced.

Hannah laughed. "Yesterday I thought I had it figured out, but today?"

"Today?" Pam prompted.

"I don't know anymore."

"Did you see anyone else yesterday?"

Hannah sat forward. “Yes, I almost forgot. Last night, around nine or so, Nellie started to bark so I let her out. A couple of kids were walking from the beach toward the cottages, but when they saw me, they ran off.”

Hannah noticed Pam’s jaw clench several times. “We’ve had some problems with partying at your place when it was empty. What did you do with the gun after you threatened Vern and Chase?”

Hannah held her hands up, palms out. “I wouldn’t call it *threaten*. I told you before, I was holding the gun when I asked them to leave. After they left? I leaned it against the cottage I was staying in and forgot about it until I saw it in your hands earlier.”

“Did you go into the other cottages?”

“I walked around and looked in the windows but I didn’t have the energy to deal with anything but getting cottage number one cleaned up enough so I could be comfortable sleeping there."

Officer Larson nodded and handed Hannah a business card. "Thank you for coming in. Here's my contact information if you think of anything else." She stared at Hannah meaningfully. "Anything."

Hannah rose from the chair and turned toward the door, but before she walked out, she pivoted. "There is one more thing I just thought of. It's probably nothing, but . . ."

Officer Larson nodded for her to continue.

"I heard a couple of loud booms this morning. Actually, the first one, more like a crack, woke me up. After I bumped into Cal, he said there was some blasting in town. The first one, the one that woke me up, sounded awfully close and different from the ones I heard when I was talking to Cal."

"Did you investigate the noise when you heard it?"

"I went outside but didn't see anything, then Nellie ran off and I followed her down the beach. At the time, Cal's explanation made sense, but now, well, I wonder if it was the gunshot I heard."

"What time was that? I can check if there was blasting going on when you heard the noise."

Hannah crunched her mouth and looked at her watch. "I didn't check the time, but working backwards, it's almost noon now, it must have been around eight when I heard the first crack?"

"Thank you Ms. Holiday. Please don't leave town." Pam opened her laptop and Hannah assumed their meeting was over.

Cal was waiting in the parking lot, talking on his cell phone. He snapped it shut when he saw Hannah walk outside.

"All set?"

She nodded.

"Pam didn't eat you for breakfast?" He checked the time. "Or lunch?"

Hannah smiled. "It was okay. Glad it's behind me."

He opened the passenger door of his pickup for Hannah, then jogged to the driver's side and climbed in. "How about we stop at my place for some lunch."

"Sure," she answered since she had no idea where else she could go until the police were done investigating her place.

Cal drove through town and turned into a parking lot.

Hannah looked at him. "This is a marina."

"Yup, it's the Bayside Marina." He parked his truck. "That's my place," he pointed, "the white boat with a blue top."

"You live on a boat?" She tried to hide the shock in her voice but was completely unsuccessful.

Cal chuckled. “Yeah, I get that reaction all the time. Uh oh, here comes Chase Fuller, the owner, probably not someone you care to bump into after your meeting with him yesterday.”

“Well, well, well. Look who my least favorite tenant dragged in.” Chase scowled at Hannah. “I hope you left your shotgun home.”

Cal grinned. “Speaking of shotguns, Chase, where were you earlier this morning?”

“What kind of stupid question is that? Were you looking for me to finally pay your rent? You know I always take my jog on the beach from eight to nine.”

“Interesting. Right about the time Vern was shot.”

Chase’s eyebrows shot up out of sight under his shaggy hair. “What are you accusing me of?” With that, he turned and stormed off, turning his head a couple of times to glare at Hannah and Cal.

Chapter 4

Cal laughed out loud. “That certainly riled him up.”

“Do you know when Vern was shot?” Hannah asked.

“Not exactly, but when I opened the door and saw him, I don’t think it could have been much more than an hour before we arrived.” Cal led Hannah down the dock to his boat. “Watch your step.” He reached for her hand but she jumped gracefully from the main dock to the back of his boat. “Go ahead into the cabin and I’ll see what I can find for us to eat.”

Hannah opened the door. The cabin was small but tidy and cozy. The left side had a long, cushy L-shaped bench seat surrounding a table on two sides. The right side of the cabin had a small counter, sink, and stove. A refrigerator was nestled under the counter. Beyond all of that, in the front of the boat was the sleeping area. You wouldn't be able to stand there, but you could sit up.

Hannah slid onto the bright blue cushioned bench seat while Cal rummaged around for food. He pulled out bread, a can of tuna fish, mayo, and pickles. "Tuna sandwich work for you?" he asked while draining the liquid from the tuna fish.

"Sure." Hannah watched him work, enjoying the thought of someone waiting on her. Especially a handsome someone. "How can you pin point when Vern was shot?"

He scooped mayo from the jar and stirred it into the tuna. "I was a premed student. Medical stuff has always fascinated me."

"You were? What happened?"

"Life." He cut the sandwiches into triangles and carried the plates to the table. He opened his half size fridge. "Water okay? Or, I do have a couple of beers in here."

"Hmmm. A beer is tempting. I'll buy you more," she offered.

Cal popped the cap off of two bottles of beer and slid into the L-shape portion of the seat, at a right angle to Hannah. He clinked his beer against hers. "Welcome to Hooks Harbor. Maybe not the best way to begin your life here, but it will be memorable!"

Hannah nodded, took a sip of the cold beer, and added, "That's one way to put it."

They ate in silence. Hannah enjoyed the gentle rocking of the boat. She appreciated Cal's company and she wanted to ask more about what got in the way of his medical schooling but decided he might not want to talk about it.

She leaned back against the cushion, wiped her lips, and asked, "You said there were other reasons someone might want to shoot Vern."

Cal took a long slug of his beer. "That's right. I guess people might think I had a motive too. Vern owed me a lot of money. Chase likes to throw my lack of cash in my face every chance he gets, but I don't let it bother me."

Hannah digested his comments.

"I can see what you're thinking. I was on the beach, did I shoot Vern?"

Hannah lowered her eyes, uncomfortable that he could read her thoughts.

"Don't worry. If I was going to kill Vern, I would have made it look like an accident. Not that I spent any time planning anything like that. He wasn't worth the time to me. Sure, I'm upset and annoyed about the money, but life's too short to ruin it over a piece of scum like him."

"Who else could have done it?"

Cal stood up, gathered the plates, and put them in the small sink. "Come on. We'll walk around town so you can meet the people who live here and decide for yourself the answer to that question."

"You don't have to chaperone me if you've got something else to do."

He waved his hand, brushing away her comment. "I'd love to start the projects at your place but I'll have to wait until the police are done there. After I show you around, I'll get an estimate together for you to look at."

They walked off the dock, through the parking lot, and headed left into the downtown area.

"It must be busy in the summer," Hannah said.

"Busy? More like overflowing with people. I prefer it like this but I understand the summer tourists are what pay the bills for just about everyone. You'll see. Your little place will be mobbed." He turned to look at

Hannah. "Do you plan to hire someone to help you?"

"Did Caroline hire anyone?"

"Yeah, she did as a matter of fact. A great woman, named Meg. Vern hired her to work at his Inn after Caroline died, but you might want to contact her and see if she's interested in her old job back. Once you get up and running, of course."

"Here's the town bookstore," Cal explained as they arrived at the beginning of the shops. "Everyone struggles a bit at this time of year but summer makes up for the slow times."

Hannah stopped in front of the window of the next shop, admiring the jewelry display which Cal explained was all made by a local silversmith. She especially loved silver, but rarely wore much jewelry. Maybe she would stop in to buy something for her sister.

As they passed the open front door of the next shop, Simply Sweets, Hannah got the intoxicating aroma of chocolate. She held Cal's arm to make him stop. "Let's go in here. I'll buy you a treat since you so kindly made lunch for me."

"Ah, a chocoholic?"

Hannah laughed. "Yes, my biggest vice."

Before walking inside, Cal whispered, "This store belongs to Vern's wife. Well, estranged wife, but I don't think they are divorced yet."

Hannah's eyebrows shot up. "Isn't it odd that the shop is open?"

A little bell jingled when Cal opened the door, letting Hannah enter first. "Let's see who's here."

The shop had a glass case filled with assorted chocolate bonbons, each one looking more delicious than anything Hannah had seen before. A taller shelf displayed chocolate shaped whales and shells. Hannah reached for a wooden box with nine whales nestled in white papers lined up neatly in three rows of three.

A ceramic shell sat on the counter filled with small pieces of chocolate samples. Hannah chose a piece of dark chocolate, letting it melt on her tongue. It was rich and creamy with a hint of orange. Exquisite.

"Can I help you?"

Hannah looked into the dark brown eyes of a teenager. Her blonde pigtails reached her shoulders and a friendly smile spread across her face.

"Hi Tasha," Cal said. "How's your mom?"

Hannah stepped aside, letting Cal continue his conversation.

The smile disappeared, replaced by a scowl. "She's fine. My stepdad got just what he deserved. Finally. Now, Mom won't have to go through a nasty divorce to get what she would have had to fight that cheap S.O.B for."

"Tasha?" an angry voice yelled from the back of the store. "I'm back from a grilling with Officer Larson. Where were you last night?"

Tasha swung her head around, pigtails flying behind her. "Mom, I'm helping customers," she answered.

A middle aged woman, dressed in a flowing colorful skirt, white blouse under a dark red vest, and a turquoise silk scarf, entered the shop from a back room and immediately pasted a smile on her face. "Hello, Cal. What brings you into my shop today? I didn't know you cared much for my fancy chocolates."

Hannah heard an underlying tone of suspicion in her voice.

"Kelley, I'm showing, Hannah Holiday, the new owner of Caroline's cottages, around town. She took a fancy to the chocolate aromas drifting out the door when we passed by your shop."

Kelley's head turned as if she only noticed Hannah for the first time. She extended her hand. "Pleased to meet you." Before Hannah could shake her hand, Kelley jerked it to cover her mouth. "You're the one who found Vern?" Her eyes were wide with shock.

"Actually, Cal found him. I'm sorry for your loss." Hannah wasn't sure what to say in the awkward situation she found herself in.

"Ha. No loss for me. Of course it's tragic, but everyone in town knows that the relationship I had with Vern was only heading in one direction. Divorce." She put her arm around her daughter's shoulder. "Heaven only knows what he was doing in one of *your* cottages."

All eyes were on Hannah after that comment. Did they think she killed him?

Hannah looked at the box of chocolates she held.

Cal took the box and placed it on the counter. "I think we're all set if you can ring this up for Hannah."

Hannah carried her bag outside. They walked away from the store before Hannah said, "That felt strange. Did it sound like Kelley suspected me of killing her husband?"

"I'm sure there will be a lot of finger pointing going on until this is solved. Don't let her bother you. In Kelley's world, it's always someone else's fault. It will be interesting to know where she was when Vern was shot."

Chapter 5

Cal dropped Hannah off at Jack's house on his way to get prices and draw up a quote for the work on the café and cottages. Nellie ran in circles when Hannah walked inside. Jack put the tea kettle on and rummaged through his cupboards, finding an unopened bag of chocolate chip cookies.

"Did Cal show you around?"

"After my chat with your daughter at the police station, he made me lunch. How long has he lived on that boat?" Hannah asked while she opened the cookies and helped herself to one.

Jack poured tea and joined her at the table. "Ever since he left medical school and moved here he's lived on that boat." Jack shrugged. "He says he likes it."

Hannah blew on her tea before taking a sip. "Why didn't he finish med school?"

"He doesn't like to talk about what can't be changed. This is what happened. His sister was in a terrible car accident and he came back to help her. They had a big argument over his decision, but when Cal makes up his mind, there's no changing it."

"Where does his sister live?"

Jack bit into a cookie. "Finish your tea and we'll take Nellie for a walk. I'll fill you in."

Jack's phone rang. Hannah could hear his side of the conversation while she drank her tea.

"Okay, Pam, I'll let her know." Jack hung up.

"Pam said if I run into you to let you know you can stay in your cottage tonight. Cottage number four still has police tape but they should finish up tomorrow."

Hannah brought her cup to the sink. "That's a relief. I can't leave town so I was thinking I'd be sleeping in Great Aunt Caroline's car."

“That old dark blue Volvo wagon? Does it even start?”

“Good question. I took the bus here from the airport. I guess I’ll have to get it to a mechanic to check it over. I’ll definitely need a car to get this business up and running again.”

Jack handed the leash to Hannah. Nellie heard the jingle and was excited to head outside. “You can let her run. She’s supposed to be on a leash on the beach, but we can risk letting her run free at this time of year.”

Nellie dashed across the road, straight to the beach, without a glance backwards. Hannah decided she would need some help training Nellie if she was going to keep her. She wanted a dog that would listen to her and not chase after any scent that blew up her nose.

Jack headed to the left which would bring them in front of Hannah's cottages. "Have you walked this way yet?"

"Nope. I have a lot of exploring to do still."

"Getting back to Cal's story, his sister's name is Monica. She's about ten years older than Cal and always watched out for him when he was growing up. From what I know, she kept him out of a lot of trouble through his teenage years."

Hannah laughed at Nellie chasing the seagulls. She threw off her flip flops and pulled up her jeans, letting the waves wash over her feet. Jumping out of the water, she screeched, "This water is cold!"

"It's December. Of course it's cold." Jack watched Hannah and Nellie cavorting on the beach. "Your Great Aunt Caroline had a lot of sense bringing you here to Hooks Harbor. You're going to make someone very happy."

Hannah scrunched her eyebrows. "What's that supposed to mean?"

Jack laughed. "Oh, nothing."

They walked in silence, Hannah digging her toes into the cold, wet sand with each step. Jack pointed to a small grey-shingled cottage. "There's someone here that you should meet."

Hannah's brain was filled with new people, new stories, and a disturbing new image. She stopped walking, trying to decide if she was up for another introduction.

Jack waved her forward. "Don't dawdle. Monica doesn't bite."

"Monica? Cal's sister?" Hannah jogged to catch up with Jack, slipping her flip flops on her almost frozen feet. She whistled to get Nellie's attention and, surprisingly, she charged after Hannah.

Hannah and Nellie followed Jack up the ramp to a porch overlooking the ocean. The porch extended the full length of the small house, increasing the house size by at least half. Jack had already made himself comfortable in a deck chair next to Monica. A small table was nestled between Monica and Jack with a Simply Sweets bag sitting next to a tea cup.

"Come on over and meet Cal's sister, Monica," Jack said as he motioned Hannah to join them. "Hannah only arrived in town yesterday," he explained.

Hannah glanced around to check on Nellie's whereabouts, only to feel her brush against her leg as she surged across the porch.

"Pull up a chair." Monica smiled at Hannah and extended her hand without standing up. Hannah blinked several times with the realization that Monica *couldn't* get up. She sat in a wheelchair. "I can tell by the shock on your face that my overprotective brother didn't tell you about this." She patted the arms of her wheelchair. Her face still held a smile but her eyes sent an unspoken warning to Hannah, *don't mess with Cal*.

Hannah sat in the offered chair, hoping Jack would make conversation since Hannah didn't have a clue where to begin. An awkward silence followed.

Hannah began to talk at the same moment Monica spoke.

"Sorry, go ahead," Hannah said.

"I'm wondering how you met Cal already." The smile stayed on her lips but her suspicious eyes searched Hannah's face.

"On the beach. Nellie," Hannah let her hand fall to pat the pup's soft head. "Nellie," she began again, "ran off down the beach yesterday morning and I took off after her. Cal was walking on the beach, heading to Jack's house."

"It was meant to be," Jack said. "I decided Cal should help Hannah fix up the café and cottages."

Hannah laughed. "You had this all planned?"

Jack shrugged. Hannah noticed a fleeting scowl cross Monica's face. Or was it her imagination?

"I can give him a stellar recommendation, although it's slightly biased," Monica said. The first genuine smile Hannah saw, appeared on Monica's face. "He remodeled this house for me after my accident. He's a genius with wood and a hammer. Such a waste, really."

"Sorry? A waste?" Hannah regretted the words as soon as they left her mouth.

Monica's lips tightened. "Yes. He should be using his brains to finish medical school, not wasting his time dealing with the likes of people like Vern Mason. Someone who treats everyone like scum and worse than that, doesn't even pay for a job well done."

Hannah felt uncomfortable with the hatred she heard in Monica's voice. Maybe she felt guilty because of Cal's choice to leave medical school. Most likely, she blamed herself. Whatever it was, Hannah knew Monica was suspicious of her. Probably of everyone.

Jack leaned forward. "Did you hear the news yet?"

"About Vern?" Monica shrugged. "I heard. No loss for sure. Someone did this town a huge favor."

"And his wife," Jack added. "She won't have to fight him in divorce court now. Pam will get to the bottom of this, no matter where it leads."

Monica checked her watch. "If you two will excuse me, I need to get ready for work. I'm working three to seven today."

"Of course." Jack stood up. "By the way, how's your beach wheelchair working out?"

Hannah glanced to the far side of the porch, noticing a chair with wide inflated tires.

"With my new ramp, and new chair, I can get to the beach on my own now. Cal had to twist my arm to get me to buy it, but don't tell him this: it's the best thing that's happened to me in a long time. I don't want to hear *I told you so*." She laughed as she pushed herself toward the big sliding doors leading into the house. "Thanks for stopping by."

Jack led the way to the beach, heading back toward Hannah's place. "Let's take a quick look at your car. See if it will start."

Hannah found a key hanging on a hook next to a small mirror in the living room of the cottage she was making her own. Jack, with his head under the raised hood and leaning in as far as possible, pulled out the oil dip stick. He pulled an old handkerchief from his pocket, wiped the dip stick, replaced it, and pulled it out again. "Surprise of surprises. The oil is clean and up to the level it should be. Maybe Caroline did maintain this car after all."

"I found this key inside."

"Well, what are you waiting for? See if it turns over."

Hannah slid into the driver's seat, inserted the key, crossed her fingers, and turned the key. The old Volvo hesitated before surging to life. Jack slammed the hood down and climbed into the passenger seat. "Let's take this big hog for a test drive. Just to my house until you get plates. I can do that for you."

Hannah reached down to adjust the seat. Her fingers searched for the lever, instead feeling an envelope. She tried to pull it out but it was stuck on something. She yanked harder until it pulled loose. Hannah turned it over in her hands. It was addressed to Vern Mason but never mailed.

Hannah looked at Jack watching her. "Go ahead and open it," he encouraged her.

With shaky fingers, feeling like her great aunt was looking over her shoulder, Hannah slit open the envelope. She unfolded the white paper neatly folded inside.

Vern. Give back the key to cottage number four. Immediately. I don't like the thought of what you are doing. Enclosed is the balance of what you already paid me. A check for five hundred dollars fell into Hannah's lap. A chill traveled up her spine.

The letter fluttered on top of the check. Jack reached for it. "Can I read it?"

Hannah nodded, still looking straight ahead through the dirty windshield. The sound of Hannah's breathing and the paper crinkling filled the car.

Jack whistled. "I can't imagine why Caroline would rent a cottage to Vern. Something smells fishier than two week old clam shells."

Hannah turned the key, silencing the engine. "Let's look around and see if we can find anything unusual."

"Where do you want to look? There's still police tape up around cottage four." Jack reached across the front seat and touched Hannah's arm. "Do you have keys for all the cottages?"

"Yes." She opened her door, letting her feet land in the soft sand. Nellie jumped over the front seat and followed Hannah out the door. She walked to cottage one, opening the office door. "I'm starting here."

Before Hannah entered the office, a truck pulled in and stopped next to the Volvo station wagon. Cal hopped out, carrying a bag. "You forgot this in my truck." He held up the bag of chocolates. "Thought you might be ready for a treat."

Jack and Cal followed Hannah inside. He set the bag on Caroline's big oak desk and looked around. "What's going on?"

Hannah opened the closet door, scanning the keys hanging on hooks. “This is interesting. There are two keys for every cottage except cottage four.” She lifted the lone key from its hook. “Maybe that explains how Vern got inside.”

Cal pointed to an empty hook. “What happened to the master key?”

“Officer Larson asked for it for her investigation.”

“You think Vern stole a key for cottage four?” Cal asked.

Hannah shook her head. “No, Caroline gave it to him. He was renting it.”

Cal’s eyes popped wide open. “What?”

Jack handed Cal the letter Hannah found under the seat of the Volvo. He stroked the stubble on his cheek as he read the words. “What was he doing in the cottage?”

“I don’t know, but whatever it was, I’ll bet this whole property that it’s the reason someone shot him.” Hannah declared.

Chapter 6

Hannah reached inside the bag Cal left on the desk. She opened the box and offered a chocolate to Cal and Jack.

"Kelley's chocolate? I can't say no to that," Jack said as he chose the center piece. "I don't like her but her chocolates are to die for."

Cal waved his hand. "None for me, thanks. I'm not a big chocolate fan."

Hannah raised her eyebrows. "How can anyone not love chocolate?" She nibbled the edge of a whale's tail, savoring the creaminess as it melted in her mouth. "I'll save the rest for later." She closed the box, leaving it on the desk. *Her* desk now, she told herself. With a key for each cottage in her pocket, she said, "Let's poke around in cottages two and three."

Officer Larson was reaching for the doorknob from the outside when Hannah pulled it open from the inside.

"Just who I'm looking for," Pam said in a neutral tone.

Hannah squished the rest of the now soft chocolate against the roof of her mouth with her tongue and swallowed. She looked over her shoulder, wondering who Pam was looking for—her, Jack, or Cal.

"Can we sit down inside?" Pam tilted her head, waiting for Hannah to reply.

Cal and Jack walked past the two women. "We'll wait outside," Jack said.

Hannah stood aside so Pam could enter. "Have a seat."

"That's not necessary. I only have a couple of questions." She slid her notebook from her back pocket and flipped through a few pages. "What time did you say you heard the loud bangs?"

Hannah rubbed her chin. "I'm not sure but I think the first crack, the one that woke me up, was around eight and the other two were around eight-thirty."

Pam nodded. "That's interesting. The blasting definitely didn't start until eight-thirty." She looked at Hannah. "Did you see anyone? Did you even look around at the cottages?"

"No. Nellie ran to the beach and I wanted to find her. Then I bumped into Cal, and we walked to Jack's house. When he told me it could be blasting, I forgot about it until—" Her voice tapered off, leaving her last thought unspoken.

"So Cal Murphy was on the beach when you heard the later bangs?"

"Yes. But I don't know when he got to the beach."

Pam jotted some notes in her notebook and tapped her lip with her index finger.

Hannah pulled Caroline's letter from her pocket. "I found this a little while ago." She handed it to Pam.

Pam looked at Hannah before sliding the letter from the envelope. "Where did you find this?" Her face was a mask, betraying no emotions.

"Stuck under the driver seat of my great aunt's Volvo. I was trying to adjust the seat and felt something stuck there."

"And this check was with the letter?"

Hannah nodded.

"What about the key?"

Hannah shrugged and walked to the closet. She pointed to the keys hanging on the door. "There were two keys for each cottage except cottage four. It doesn't prove that Vern had the extra key, but it's missing."

"If you find anything else, let me know. Take a look through Caroline's books and see if you can find when Vern gave her a check. If he wrote a check. If he was doing something shady, he might have paid with cash. I'm taking the police tape down so you can get back to work. Oh, and it might be a good idea to change the locks since we didn't find a key for cottage four on Vern or in the cottage." Pam started to walk away but turned back to Hannah. "Are you sure you're up for the challenges of running this business?" she asked before heading to cottage number four, not waiting for an answer.

Hannah stood in front of her office, letting that question cloud her brain. She had managed to keep her insecurities at bay but Pam brought them front and center. No, she wasn't at all sure she was cut out for what was ahead. She wondered what the story was with Pam. And she wondered what Cal was doing at the beach so early yesterday morning. Coincidence? Or something else?

Her stomach sank when she saw that Jack and Cal had the hood up on the Volvo.

"Did you find something wrong with the car?" she asked when she reached them.

"Nope," Cal said with a big smile across his face. "Looks like Caroline took good care of her car. You shouldn't have a lick of trouble."

"What's up with my daughter? She's acting like she got up on the wrong side of the bed this morning," Jack said after he slammed the hood closed.

"She had a few more questions for me."

"Did you show her the letter?"

"Uh huh. She didn't react. I can't get a read on her except that she doesn't think I'm cut out to run this place." Hannah's eyes moved between Jack and Cal, hoping for some kind of positive feedback.

Jack chuckled. "Don't let her get under your skin. She's probably upset that I have a new friend. And a good looking one at that." He winked at Hannah and lowered his voice. "She's never been good in the sharing department. It's probably why she's divorced, but don't tell her I said that."

Pam returned to her car with a trash bag filled with the police tape from cottage number four. "We're all done here." She tossed it into the back seat of her cruiser before turning to face Jack. "Dad, have you seen Noah recently?"

"He hasn't stopped by my house, if that's what you mean. I did see him hanging out with a bunch of his friends yesterday. They were sitting on the town green, bored and looking for trouble. Why?"

Her jaw muscles worked furiously. "I'll stop by later and talk to you about him. I'm worried."

Jack nodded and waved as she drove out.

"That son of hers. I don't know the kids he's hanging around with, except one girl—

Vern's stepdaughter, Tasha. He's got it bad for her and I don't think it sits well with Pam. Ya know, the sharing thing again."

"Tasha? From Simply Sweets?" Hannah asked.

"Yup, that's the one. So, Hannah, are you ready for a tour around town now? I'll get my car," Jack said.

"Great idea," Cal agreed. "You can pick out your new appliances for cottage one. I'll have it all transformed for you in less than a week."

Hannah smiled. The thought of her own cozy place on the beach felt good. Whatever else was coming her way was pushed to the background. Instead, she imagined a gleaming counter in her new kitchen, shiny wood floors, and a porch overlooking the ocean.

She looked at her cottage and pointed. "Cal, can you build a deck on the ocean side of my cottage? Like the one at your sister's place? Maybe not as big, but I'd like it to wrap around this side so I can sit outside with my feet up and watch the sunrise over the ocean. And have it extend to the office side. The office porch should have a ramp, too," she added, thinking of accommodating any handicapped guests.

Cal nodded enthusiastically. "I tried to convince Caroline to add a deck but she said it was too frivolous. It's a great idea and it will be like adding another room, at least when the weather is nice."

Jack pulled in with his window down and made a big deal of checking his watch. "Come on you two. If you want to find your new appliances today, we'd better get a move on." He climbed from his car. "You drive so you get a better feel for the town," Jack said to Hannah, not giving her a chance to decline the offer.

Cal opened the back door, letting Nellie jump in first, and he tucked his long legs behind the passenger seat. "Hey Jack. Slide your seat up so I have a little more room back here."

Jack did as he was asked.

Hannah maneuvered onto the street. "Someone needs to tell me where we're going." She turned her head to make a quick glance at Jack next to her.

Cal took charge and directed her through town, pointing out various businesses. He offered a little background and suggested, what he considered, to be the best places for Hannah to shop. "Pull in here. This isn't your big box store but Al carries quality and he has decent prices. He'll give me a discount as your contractor, too."

Cal suggested particular appliances, considering price and features. He narrowed the choices down to a couple, letting Hannah make the final decision. It was a lot to process and became a blur for her. She was thankful that Cal knew what he was doing and she trusted him to get the best prices for her.

“Okay,” Cal said when they were back on the street. “I’ll pick everything up with my truck to save on a delivery charge.” He looked at Hannah. “What’s next?”

Hannah looked at Jack for suggestions. “How about we take a drive up the coast. Hannah should have a feel for the area so she can make recommendations to her renters.”

Oceanside Drive meandered past weathered homes, various restaurants, and numerous gift shops. “You should make a list in case anyone asks you for suggestions. Also, it wouldn’t be a bad idea to try a few restaurants before you recommend them,” Jack advised.

“Do you think you can find your way back without our help?” Cal asked.

Hannah reached into her small canvas tote bag and pulled out her smart phone. She punched in her address. "Sure. I live in the modern world, you know."

Jack chuckled. "What will you do when your phone dies?"

She pulled out her car phone charger. "I guess you've resisted the modern conveniences," Hannah teased.

Her phone directed her to turn around and follow Oceanside Drive back to Hooks Harbor. They all laughed out loud. Hannah said, "Even I could have figured this out."

As they drove through town, Jack told Hannah to pull over at the town center. "You two wait here, okay? I want to talk to Noah for a minute."

Cal and Hannah chatted easily. He told her about the upcoming Christmas by the Sea Celebration which included a Clam Chowder Cook Off. "It pulls in a lot of visitors which helps businesses at this time of year. And it's a lot of fun." He asked,

"You've never come here before? Even when you were younger?"

"We used to come until I was about twelve." She shrugged. "Caroline and my father had a falling out. Communication broke off between her and my dad, her only nephew. I don't even know what all the drama was about. Caroline kept in touch with me over the years, much to the irritation of my father."

"Why did she leave her place to you?"

Hannah shrugged. "Everyone told me I look like her, at least when she was younger. I think she wanted to annoy my folks. And, it was either going to me or my sister Ruby, but she has a career and wouldn't be able to uproot as easily."

Jack got back into the car, slamming the door. "Such rudeness. Since when did this younger generation become so hostile to their elders?"

"He's eighteen? It's a difficult age with everyone asking what you're going to do with the rest of your life. Heck, I'm still trying to figure that out and I'm already twenty seven!" She laughed, trying to lighten the mood for Jack's sake.

"It's a difficult age all right, and if he doesn't figure something out, he won't have to worry about what he'll be doing for the rest of his life."

Silence filled the car. Hannah couldn't help but think about the teenagers she saw on the beach the night before Vern was shot. What were they doing? Just looking for a place to hang out and get drunk? Or something more sinister?

Hannah parked Jack's car next to Cal's truck in front of her cottage. Another car was parked to the side and she could see someone standing on the beach looking out over the ocean.

"Are you expecting company?" Cal asked.

Hannah puckered her lips. “No, but my life has been filled with the unexpected lately, so why not one more event for the day.”

When she slammed the car door closed, the woman on the beach turned around and waved. She held the hand of a child. Her short brown hair blew around, covering her face. Hannah squinted, trying to figure out if she knew this person or if she was only being friendly.

Suddenly, she put two and two together. Running to the beach with Nellie hot on her heels, Hannah embraced the woman and they stood joined together, squealing and doing a happy dance for several minutes.

Chapter 7

Hannah picked up the little girl and twirled her around in circles. They both screeched and laughed.

“I can’t believe you’re here, Olivia.” Hannah set her niece down, keeping hold of her hand, and wrapped her other arm around her sister Ruby. She looked at Jack and Cal watching her. “Come on.” She started walking back toward the cottages. “What a surprise,” Hannah said, still in shock that her sister showed up out of the blue.

“Really Hannah? You’re surprised? I heard about the murder on the news and you never called to tell me you arrived safely. You haven’t answered my messages. What is going on?” Ruby scolded her younger sister.

“Yeah, the murder. Everything’s been so crazy since I arrived. Sorry, I should have known you’d be worried, but without a T.V.

blasting constant coverage of the murder in my face, I guess I forgot you would hear about it."

They walked through the sand in silence except for Olivia, now walking and holding Hannah's hand. She chattered away happily to Nellie. "My name is Olivia but you can call me Liv. What's your name?"

Hannah laughed. "Olivia, the dog's name is Nellie. Isn't she adorable?"

Ruby glared. "She's allergic, you know."

"Mommy, I *luv* Nellie. Are we going to stay here with Aunt Hannah and Nellie?"

"We'll see, dear."

"You've got your first company, Hannah. What a surprise," Jack said.

Hannah introduced Ruby and Olivia to Jack and Cal.

Cal crouched down, petting Nellie while he talked to Olivia. "Hi, my name is Cal. I see you have a new friend already."

Olivia's face lit up and her grin went from ear to ear. She wrapped her arms around Nellie's neck who was a good sport and didn't squirm too much. Instead, her head twisted toward Olivia and her tongue traveled from Olivia's chin to her forehead.

Ruby picked her daughter up. "Hannah, where can I wash her up before she breaks out in a rash?"

Hannah rolled her eyes. "Don't worry about her so much. Let her be a kid and enjoy herself. Let's pull some chairs outside so we can enjoy the rest of this sunny afternoon. I don't imagine this mild weather will last for the whole winter."

Ruby let out a deep sigh. "Okay. That's probably the only way I'll get you to fill me in on what's going on around here."

Hannah said a silent thank you that Cal and Jack weren't deserting her. As much as she loved her sister, she knew Ruby arrived with an agenda and it probably wasn't a good one. Ruby always knew what was best for Hannah, at least she thought she did, and Hannah was definitely not up for any battles with everything else that was suddenly on her plate.

Cal found four chairs and a small rocker just the right size for Olivia. Olivia had other things on her mind though, like chasing Nellie or pushing sand around into big piles once Nellie flopped down for a snooze.

Hannah brought out a tray with glasses and a pitcher of water. "This is all I've got at the moment. I haven't had a chance to stock up my kitchen yet. And, since Cal will be gutting it to do the upgrades, I'll probably just eat out until all the work is done."

"You've only been here for, what, a day and a half? Are you moving forward too quickly?" Ruby asked after she gulped down half a glass of water.

"I want to be open for business as soon as possible."

"I can't believe Great Aunt Caroline disrupted your life like this. Hannah, what about your plans for graduate school? A real career, instead of—" she waved her hand around, "instead of this, this, these rundown shacks in a pile of sand."

Hannah laughed. "Don't mince any words. You sound just like Dad." She turned to face Ruby straight on and her face turned serious. "What's wrong with having my own business? Look out at the view. You can't tell me looking out and listening to the ocean isn't almost magical. We were never allowed to get to know Great Aunt Caroline, but since I've been here for this day and a half, I've been thanking her for every minute." Hannah sat back in her chair. Every minute except for the dead body part, but she wasn't going to admit *that* to her sister.

Ruby sighed again. "I wonder if you'll be singing this same song once reality hits you and you actually have to make money here and deal with renters and make all those pots of clam chowder and crab rolls and lobster whatever it was that Caroline sold in her snack bar." Ruby snorted with disdain. "Great Aunt Caroline didn't leave you enough money to live in your dream world forever."

Hannah decided not to respond. There was no point egging Ruby on since Ruby always had the last word. Instead, she came up with a different strategy. "Why are you here? How could you up and leave your job so easily?"

Ruby looked down at the empty glass in her hand. "I got fired. Two weeks ago. I didn't want to worry you."

Hannah's hand flew over to stroke her sister's arm. "Fired?" What Hannah didn't say out loud was that she knew her sister could be difficult and this wasn't the first time she had been fired. A pattern was emerging but Ruby always said it was someone else's fault. She shook her head, realizing her sister was talking to her.

". . . so I can stay here and help you." Ruby looked at Hannah. "Were you listening to me?"

"Yeah, yeah. Stay here and help me, you said." Hannah scratched her forehead, trying to figure out how to let her down gently.

Cal leaned forward. "How about your sister stays in cabin number four. Once all the blood gets cleaned up."

The color drained from Ruby's face. "Blood? What are you talking about? You know I hate the thought of blood."

Hannah patted her hand. "The murder you heard about? What exactly did the news say?"

"Just the guy's name, owner of some Inn, was murdered in Hooks Harbor. Why?" She looked first at Hannah, then at Cal.

"Well, he was murdered in the cottage over there." Hannah pointed to the last cottage—cottage number four.

Ruby stood up. "You can't stay here. It's not safe. What if the murderer comes back?"

"I have a gun. Well, I did have a gun but the police officer took it. It's the murder weapon." Hannah was starting to enjoy this side benefit of Vern's death right under her nose. There was no way her sister would be staying *here* and bothering her.

"A gun? Since when do you carry guns?" Ruby was standing with her arms flailing around. "What has happened to you? I don't talk to you for a couple of weeks and you've become someone I don't even know anymore."

"Please. Stop the hysteria. I don't 'carry guns' as you put it. It's Caroline's gun. I found it in her cottage—mine now."

Olivia called to her mother, "Mommy, look what I found. Can I keep it?"

"What is it honey?" Ruby put her hand out. Olivia held up a gold chain with a medallion.

Jack stood up and moved closer to Ruby. "Can I take a look at that?" He studied it after Ruby dropped it in his hand. "This belongs to my grandson, Noah. I wonder how it got here." He looked at Ruby. "I'll have to show this to my daughter. Okay?"

Ruby nodded. "Olivia, honey, it belongs to someone else. Thanks for finding it."

"I'll take you to a store in town so you can pick out something for yourself instead,"

Hannah offered. "There's a local silversmith and she makes beautiful jewelry."

"Can we go now?" Olivia asked, jumping and clapping her hands.

Hannah looked at Ruby. "Feel like a change of scenery? And you can find a room in town, too."

Ruby nodded. "I think that's exactly what I need."

"I'll make you three ladies," Cal made a point to include Olivia, "dinner on my boat if you'd like."

Hannah nodded her agreement. Ruby hesitated. Olivia twirled in circles until she fell in a heap.

"We'll be there at six, or a little earlier if we get done shopping. I'll bring some beer to replace what I drank at lunch time," Hannah said, making a decision before Ruby could come up with an excuse.

“Great. Nothing fancy. You saw the size of my kitchen,” Cal reminded Hannah as he climbed into his truck.

She waved to Cal.

“What a whirlwind,” Ruby said. “Are you up for all this?”

“Funny you should ask. The police officer asked me the same thing. I was having my doubts, but not anymore. It’s funny, but I feel like I’m home.” She grabbed her sister’s arm and Olivia’s hand. “Let’s see what we can find in town.”

After Olivia was safely buckled into her car seat and Ruby was sitting behind the wheel, Hannah walked Jack around the back of the car. “You look worried. Is it about the gold chain?”

“Yes. Noah always wears it. I don’t know what this means but, yes, I’m very worried. For him.”

Chapter 8

Ruby started her rental car. "Tell me the way."

Hannah smiled to herself. That was exactly what she said earlier when she went out with Jack and Cal. Now, she was already the guide. Quick learning curve. She directed Ruby to town with no trouble and they parked on the street.

"A little walking will give you a chance to do some window shopping. And we can enjoy all the Christmas decorations on the shops." Hannah held onto Olivia's hand as the little girl skipped beside her, jumping over any cracks in the sidewalk.

"Here we are. The jewelry store. I haven't been inside yet, but look at the display in the window."

Hannah and Ruby feasted their eyes on the beautiful handcrafted jewelry but Olivia pulled Hannah's hand trying to get her to the door.

"Come on," she whined. "You promised."

As they entered the store, a bell over the door tinkled. Hannah held Olivia's hand tightly so she didn't have the freedom to dash around the store and knock anything over. That wasn't a concern. Olivia was drawn like a moth to a low table filled with necklaces and bracelets made especially for little girls. There were even smooth colorful rocks.

Olivia examined everything before picking up a blue stone, polished to a smooth finish. She held it in both of her tiny hands, rubbing it between her palms. "This one." She held it up for Hannah to see. "This is the one I want." Her big brown eyes stared at Hannah with a childish innocence.

"Perfect," Hannah said. "That's the prettiest stone I've ever seen. You hold on to it until your mom is done picking out something for herself."

Ruby was mesmerized by the earring display, turning the stand around and around until she chose silver earrings with pieces of blue sea glass dangling on a delicate silver strand. She held them up to her ears. "What do you think?" she asked her sister.

Hannah nodded approvingly. "Beautiful." She paid for the earrings and Olivia's stone.

Back on the street, she guided Ruby and Olivia into the next shop. The chocolate shop. Maybe not such a good idea, she thought as the smells made her mouth water. She didn't want to ruin everyone's appetite before they got to Cal's boat.

"How about we pick out something to have *after* dinner," she said. "That way we can share with Cal, too."

"Yeah, yeah, yeah," Olivia agreed. She pointed to chocolate covered candy canes. "Can we get those?"

Hannah looked at Ruby before answering. Ruby shrugged so Hannah waited her turn to pay while Ruby and Olivia went outside. She bought four of the chocolate covered candy canes, two milk chocolate and two dark chocolate.

Hannah handed Tasha the money. "Interesting medallion you have. Does Noah have one like that?"

Tasha's hand clutched the jewelry, quickly tucking it under her shirt. "Why do you ask?"

"I found one like it earlier today," Hannah said in a quiet, soothing tone. "His grandfather said it belonged to Noah."

A look of panic flashed across Tasha's face, gone almost before it was even there. She handed the bag of candy canes to Hannah without looking in her eyes. "It couldn't be his," she stated, but a slight shake in her voice exposed her uncertainty.

Tasha's mother entered the shop from the back of the store. "I'll take over now, Tasha," she said cheerfully. "You can restock the gift card display."

Tasha walked to an unopened box and carried it to a tall card rack. Her shoulders were tense and she held her arms close to her sides. The glance she shot at her mother was filled with hostility.

Hannah filed her observations away, determined to ask Jack or Cal more about these dynamics. Especially Jack since his grandson, apparently, was in love with this girl.

"Ms. Holiday?" Kelley Mason said in a syrupy voice. "Do you have a minute?"

Hannah looked through the front window to check on Ruby and Olivia but she couldn't see them. "A minute, but I need to catch up with my sister." She pointed outside.

Kelley approached Hannah, placing her hand on Hannah's arm. "This is a bit awkward, but I can't let Vern's death interfere with business, now can I?" Not pausing for an answer to the question, she continued, "I know Vern had a deal with Caroline to buy her property and I'd like to renegotiate the terms. Well, your property now, I guess." She looked expectantly at Hannah.

Hannah, knowing where this conversation was headed, chose to play dumb and make Kelley squirm for information.

Silence as the two women stared at each other. Kelley looked away, licking her lips and tapping the heel of her foot.

"Right. I'll just cut to the chase here. I'm prepared to make you a generous offer. You don't look like the type of person cut out for running a business on the beach."

The hairs on Hannah's neck stood up. She controlled her face to hide her anger. Instead, she smiled sweetly. "What kind of person *is* cut out for the business?" She had learned a long time ago, the best way to have this type of conversation was to throw a question right back at the other person. Take control and don't let them see their rude behavior get under your skin.

Kelley's cheeks had a slight tinge of pink when she looked at Hannah. She waved her hand dismissively. "Oh, don't take it the wrong way, dear," she said condescendingly, "but you are a bit young."

Hannah smiled again. "It must be quite convenient for you now with your husband out of the way."

Kelley's eyes popped open and darkened to almost black. "My husband and I may not have seen eye to eye on many things but we had a strong business relationship. I'm only continuing the negotiations he started with Caroline."

"Just out of curiosity, Ms. Mason, where were you yesterday morning around eight o'clock?"

Kelley leaned right into Hannah's face, causing her to tilt as far backward as possible. She sneered, "What are you implying?"

"What are you hiding?" Hannah said, refusing to let this rude person intimidate her. "Where *were* you? It should be a simple question to answer." Hannah straightened, moving herself into Kelley's personal space.

"Don't expect Chase Fuller to make you a better offer. He's got some financial difficulties at the moment." She spun around and hustled to the back office.

Hannah watched the well-groomed woman disappear, slowing her breathing to calm her nerves. Now she was even more curious as to Kelley Mason's whereabouts.

An unanswered question left many possibilities. Did she kill her husband?

Laughter erupted by the card display. "Good one, Hannah. You told her. Not many people stand up to her bullying, except my stepdad. They were two peas in a pod. They thought they could bully Caroline into selling but, you know what? Caroline played them against each other to her amusement."

Hannah moved across the shop and stood closer to Tasha. "And how did you fit into their plans? Were you in the middle of your stepdad and your mom?"

Tasha shrugged. "I hated my stepdad but I figured out how to make it work for me."

The shop door opened. Ruby and Olivia walked inside. "Aunt Hannah, come *on*," Olivia whined. "I want to go to the *boat*."

"Yup. Let's go."

Hannah made a quick stop at the liquor store for the beer she promised to bring. She added a bottle of red wine, too, for her sister who wasn't a beer drinker. She parked in the Bayside Marina lot and pointed out Cal's boat to her niece and sister.

"Looks cramped to me," Ruby said.

Hannah didn't let the jab affect her. "I prefer to think of it as cozy." Hannah held Olivia's hand as they headed down the dock toward Cal's boat.

Chase was heading in their direction. "Well, well. Ms. Holiday. What a nice surprise to see you again." He casually leaned against one of the dock uprights, arms crossed and one leg crossed over the other. "Are you interested in renting a boat slip?"

"You didn't buy a boat already, did you, Hannah?" Ruby asked in disbelief.

Hannah ignored her sister. "As a matter of fact, Chase, I'm very curious where you were yesterday morning around eight o'clock. I asked Kelley Mason and she never did give me an answer. Were you running on the beach near my cottages by any chance?"

"That is the route I take every morning, but I'm not sure what your interest is in *my* whereabouts."

"As you recall, and as I told the police, I overheard you tell Vern nothing would get in the way of you buying my property." She leveled her gaze on Chase.

Chase smirked. "And it was *your* gun that killed him, so I don't think my words can mean a whole lot in the big scheme of things. Maybe you'll need to sell that property to pay for a good lawyer." He laughed and unfolded his arms. He patted her on the shoulder as if they were buddies. "Be sure to ask your friend Cal why *he* was on the beach yesterday morning." Chase laughed again and continued down the dock in the opposite direction than Hannah was heading.

Ruby grabbed Hannah's arm. "Are you going to be arrested? You should sell that property before it ruins your life. It must be worth a fortune."

Hannah stopped and faced her sister directly. "Listen Ruby, I'm not selling. I can't, even if I wanted to with the way Caroline set up the inheritance. As far as the murder goes, I don't think I'll be arrested. Yes, the murder weapon belonged to Caroline and I did pick up the gun. Some people could think I threatened Vern and Chase the night before Vern was shot, but I was only holding the gun when I asked them to get off my property. And besides, what kind of motive do I have? There was a lot of tension between Vern, the dead guy, and the jerk I was just talking to. It seems that a lot of people with a bone to pick with Vern were either near my cottage or they don't have an alibi at the time he was shot."

"That guy," she nodded her head in the direction Chase had disappeared. "He said Cal was on the beach yesterday morning. Does *he* have a motive?"

"Vern owed Cal a lot of money for renovations to his Inn. Vern refused to pay, but that's all I know. You should book a room there and see if you can weasel some information from the employees. It's called the Paradise Inn. As far as I know, his estranged wife, Kelley Mason, will be inheriting the Inn."

Ruby stepped back, almost losing her footing and falling into the water before Hannah pulled her back to safety. "You want me to do some *spying*?" Ruby's eyes blinked several times before her lips turned up at the edges into the beginning of a smile.

Olivia's fingers slipped out of Hannah's hand as she dashed down the dock to Cal. He scooped her up and carried her onto his boat as her happy chattering drifted back to Hannah and Ruby.

Hannah's hand stopped Ruby from continuing. "Before we join them, I just want to say, let's keep our spy plan a secret between the two of us." She raised one eyebrow waiting for Ruby to answer.

"Don't you trust Cal?" she whispered.

Hannah sighed. "I want to, but the fact is, I barely know him and he *was* on the beach yesterday morning. At this point, let's trust each other and no one else until we are one hundred percent positive we can."

"So we shouldn't have dinner with him?" Ruby asked.

"Of course we should. I didn't say we couldn't hang out with him, and besides, he can fill us in on the people in town."

"Are you sure hanging out with him doesn't have anything to do with those ocean blue, save me from drowning in them, eyes?" Ruby asked.

Heat spread across Hannah's checks. She turned her head away from Ruby so she wouldn't see that her comment hit a nerve. A nerve Hannah wasn't ready to admit to herself. Yet.

"That's another reason we have to be careful." Hannah had been hurt by a handsome man before and she didn't want to make the same mistake twice. Especially if there was a chance that this handsome man might be a killer. "He's a good resource. Same with Jack. But we shouldn't blindly trust anyone. We need to be smart and careful."

Ruby shivered and bumped her shoulder into Hannah's. "This could be exciting. I could use some excitement in my life right about now."

"It could be dangerous. Don't forget that for one minute," Hannah reminded her sister.

Chapter 9

Delicious smells drifted from Cal's boat as they got closer. Olivia's giggling made Hannah smile. She was thrilled to have Olivia around even though it meant she would have to work on her relationship with Ruby. But if Ruby did stay in Hooks Harbor at the Inn, the extra pair of eyes and ears could come in handy.

Hannah helped Ruby step on to the back of the boat. She didn't want to risk another near miss of Ruby falling off the dock or overboard into the frigid Atlantic. She'd never hear the end of *that* disaster.

"Hello ladies," Cal said as they ducked their heads and entered his tight quarters. "I have an amazing helper tonight." He waved one hand in Olivia's direction. She sat on a big blue pillow, dipping corn chips into a bowl of humus, focused on her snack and not on the adult conversation.

"How did Cal know your favorite snack, Livy?" Ruby asked her daughter.

"I told him," she said in that matter of fact way that the young can. She stuffed another chip in her mouth and used her tongue to find the stray humus on her lip.

"Have a seat and help yourselves to the snacks. Pizza is in the oven, loaded with all kinds of toppings." He checked the timer. "Another fifteen minutes and we'll be in business."

Hannah set her bags on the table. "Do you have glasses? I brought beer and wine."

Olivia piped up, "And dessert. Don't forget the candy canes."

Cal raised one eyebrow as he set glasses on the table. "Candy canes. How did you know my favorite dessert?" he teased.

"Well, none for you, then, with that tone," Hannah teased right back.

Hannah poured herself a beer and a glass of wine for Ruby, letting Cal make his own beverage choice. He grabbed a beer, twisted off the top, and took a long swallow. He held the bottle up in Hannah's direction. "Thanks. For the beer and the company."

When Hannah slid onto the bench next to Ruby, her hand crunched on top of some papers. As she picked them up to move them out of the way, she couldn't help but see, in big black bold letters, 'EVICTION NOTICE IF RENT IS NOT PAID BY THE END OF THE MONTH.'

She held the paper up and glanced at Cal. "Chase is going to evict you? How far behind is your rent? If you don't mind my asking," she hurriedly added.

Cal waved his hand, dismissing the question. "I'll be fine. Kelley contacted me to do some work for her on the Inn now that she is its sole owner. I informed her it was out of the question because of Vern's unpaid bill and she said she'd take care of it. So," he raised both hands, palms up, "money problem solved. My sister will be happy to hear that and she might even stop nagging me about my career choice." He smiled. "Don't worry, your work is still at the top of my list." He set his empty beer bottle on the counter and helped himself to a second one.

Ruby knocked her knee into Hannah's. Hannah didn't dare look at her sister. She knew what was going through her head because Hannah had the same thought. With Vern dead, Cal would get paid. Did he kill Vern to get his money? Possibly, if he was desperate enough, and this eviction notice certainly could be seen as a motive. She tried to push the thought aside, telling herself it was most likely a coincidence.

"Who wants the grand tour of my boat?" The corners of Cal's eyes wrinkled.

“I do. I do,” Olivia shouted and crawled over her mother to get out of the seat. “Is there an upstairs?”

“Sort of,” Cal replied. He took her hand. “Climb up this ladder and you’ll be in my bedroom.”

Olivia scooted up the ladder like a little monkey. “Wow. I can see the ocean through the windows.” Her face got serious. “Do you ever get sick when the boat bounces around? I got sick once when Mommy took me on a boat and I threw up all over her.”

Cal laughed. “No, the bouncing doesn’t bother me, but I’ll be sure to remember to keep you on dry land when there’s a storm.”

Olivia held up a stuffed teddy bear. “Is this yours?”

Hannah laughed out loud when she saw Cal’s face turn a deep shade of pink. The teddy bear in question was so thread bare, he only had patches of fur on his cheeks.

"That's Theodore and he's just as old as I am. Thirty. I think I've aged a bit better, though." He tilted his head, looking at Hannah and Ruby for confirmation, his blue eyes catching the light coming from the strand of white Christmas lights strung above their heads. "I take him everywhere."

That admittance from the handsome, rugged man looking at her, made Hannah smile and rethink if he could possibly be a murderer. Who keeps their childhood stuffed animal forever? A sensitive person, not a killer.

"Don't laugh, Hannah. Theodore knows everything about me. I worry that someone will steal him and force him to reveal all my secrets." Cal's face was serious, but his lips twitched at the corners. "Actually, my biggest secret is that I still have him. I don't share that with many people. It makes me look kind of wimpy."

Olivia was talking to Theodore, whispering *her* secrets to the stuffed bear. "I hope we stay here. I like Cal and the boat and the chocolate candy canes and Nellie and most of all, I like holding Hannah's hand."

Hannah's eyes misted over. She hugged her sister and whispered in her ear. "You are *so* lucky."

Ruby squeezed Hannah's hand.

The timer buzzed, bringing them back to the subject of their rumbling stomachs. Olivia climbed down the ladder with Theodore tucked under her arm.

The pizza smelled amazing and looked phenomenal. Cal had mounded mushrooms, broccoli, and diced tomatoes over pesto and mozzarella. A sprinkling of feta cheese topped it all off.

"Hope you girls like a veggie pizza. I needed to use up what was in my little fridge." He pushed his pizza wheel through the crust, cutting it into eight slices. "It's hot. I'll slide a piece onto your plates."

Cal slipped into the space next to Olivia and Theodore. "Dig in so we can get to those delicious candy canes for dessert." He winked at Olivia.

Ruby took a bite and cheese stretched between the pizza to her mouth. After she managed to get it all where it belonged, she prompted Cal, "Hannah told me she met you on the beach yesterday morning."

Hannah jabbed Ruby's side with her elbow.

Cal smiled. "Lucky me. It's not often that I run into a cute," he paused to sip his beer, "a cute puppy during my morning beach walk." He took another sip and locked his eyes into Hannah's. "Followed by a beautiful woman jogging barefoot in December. Yes, it was my lucky day for sure."

"You walk on the beach every morning?" Ruby asked.

Cal kept his eyes on Hannah. "I try to, and after Jack told me about his new neighbor, I was hoping to bump into that new neighbor."

Ruby ignored Hannah's not so subtle jabs and continued her line of questioning. "What about the murder? Did you hear the gunshot?"

"No. I think with the constant crashing of waves and the sand and rocks between me and the cottages, the sound must have been muffled." Cal turned his attention to Ruby. "Where are you staying tonight? Did you get a room at the Paradise Inn?"

"Oh dear," Ruby said. "We got busy doing other things. Do you think there will still be a vacancy?"

Cal picked up his phone. "I'll give them a call for you. How many nights?"

"I'm not sure, but two anyway." She looked at Hannah. "What do you think?"

"Two is a good start."

"Reception is spotty here at the marina but I know where the hot spot is. I'll be right back." Cal jumped from the boat to the dock and walked halfway to shore before stopping to make his call.

Hannah glared at her sister. "What were you doing asking all those questions?"

"You were turning into a big piece of mush with all his talk about Theodore and meeting a beautiful woman. We have to find out more about him. And the only way to do that is to ask direct, no nonsense questions."

Hannah rolled her eyes and said under her breath, "Two days may be one too many."

Before Ruby could respond to the comment that was made just loud enough for her to hear, Cal ducked back inside the boat.

"All set. Meg is working tonight and she'll take care of you when you get to the Inn."

"Meg? Have I heard that name already?" Hannah said, more to herself, wrinkling up her lips as she tried to remember.

"I think I told you about her. She used to work for Caroline. Fantastic person. I don't think she likes working at the Inn, so if you're planning to hire any help, she's the person for you. At any rate, you can meet her and see what you think when Ruby checks in."

The pizza was gone and they all sat back and sighed contentedly. Except for Olivia. "Where did you put the candy canes, Aunt Hannah?"

Hannah stacked the plates and put them in the small sink. "I'll wash up and then we can have dessert."

Cal tried to push her away. "Don't worry about that. We can take our dessert and walk around the marina. I'll clean up later."

Hannah gave Ruby a look as if to say, can you believe this guy? She took the candy canes and followed the others off the boat to the dock.

"Who wants milk chocolate and who wants dark?"

Olivia reached up. "The sweetest one, please."

Cal said, "I'm with Olivia, milk chocolate, please."

Hannah tilted her head. "Dark for you and me, then, Ruby."

Cal led the way, nibbling on his chocolate covered candy cane while Olivia held his other hand and skipped along his side.

Ruby whispered to Hannah, "You've been replaced. Are you jealous?"

"Not in the least. A man who loves kids? Nothing wrong with *that* picture!"

Cal led them to a bench with a view between the boats to the ocean beyond. It was a peaceful and beautiful spot. Cal broke the silence. “This is what makes living on the boat worth it.”

Olivia yawned and climbed onto her mother’s lap. “We’d better get to the Inn before she falls asleep.”

Cal walked them back to the rental car. “See you tomorrow? Bright and early?”

Hannah nodded.

It was only about ten minutes to the Inn but Olivia couldn’t keep her eyes open. Hannah carried Olivia, and Ruby lugged their bags to the office.

A sturdy, middle-aged woman looked up when they opened the door. “Hannah Holiday?”

“That would be me,” Hannah answered. “This is my sister Ruby and her daughter, Olivia. Cal called earlier about a room for Ruby? He talked to Meg.”

“Yes, I’m Meg and I’m thrilled to meet anyone related to Caroline.” She vigorously shook Hannah's hand. "Caroline was a wonderful person, and she was always talking about you, Hannah. It's too bad you didn't make it here before she died." She took a key off a rack. "Follow me, I'll show you to your room."

As they trailed behind Meg, Hannah asked, "Are you working for Vern's wife, Kelley, now?"

Meg stopped dead in her tracks. "That's an odd question for a newcomer to town. Why are you interested in Kelley?" She continued up the stairs to the second floor of the Inn and unlocked the door to room number twenty. "This room on the end has the best view of the ocean," Meg said, as she opened the drapes and looked at Ruby. "I'm sure you and your daughter will be comfortable here."

Olivia, eyes suddenly open wide, bounced on the bed and Ruby put her suitcase on the dresser. "Pick us up in the morning for breakfast?" Ruby asked Hannah.

"Yeah. I'll swing by around eight."

Hannah followed Meg out. As they walked down the stairs, Meg quietly said, "I need to talk to you about Vern. He was up to something at the cottages." They continued to the office door. Meg pulled it open, turned, and asked, "Where are you staying?"

"In Caroline's cottage."

"I'll pick you up when I get off work in an hour."

Hannah felt a shot of adrenaline surge through her body. Did Meg know who killed Vern?

Chapter 10

Hannah drove through town, back to her cottage on the beach. She walked the short distance to Jack's house, excited to see Nellie. Nellie's carefree personality was the perfect antidote to the seriousness of the situation Hannah found herself being sucked into. What she wouldn't give to be able to sit back, relax, and read a riveting mystery. Instead, she was *in* a mystery.

When Hannah knocked, Jack hollered, "The door's unlocked."

Nellie woofed but turned into a wiggly fur ball as soon as Hannah made it inside. "Did you miss me?" Hannah crouched down and asked Nellie.

Jack replied, "Not really. I was almost asleep in my comfy chair."

"Sorry." Hannah looked at Jack, wondering why he was being such a grump.

"Not me. I was telling you what Nellie was saying."

Hannah chuckled. "Oh, right. Shall I take her home with me?"

"She's your dog."

Hannah sat across from Jack. "What's going on? And don't say 'oh nothing', like a typical man, I can tell something's bothering you."

Jack's eyebrows disappeared under the brim of his baseball cap. "A typical man? What do you know about *that* subject, young lady?"

"Umm, well, that slipped out by accident, I guess. I sounded like my mom when I said it. And I'm not *her* so forget I even said what I said."

"You're forgiven. Now, tell me about your dinner with Cal."

Hannah realized Jack, very tactfully, diverted the discussion away from his problems but she wasn't going to pry since it probably wasn't any of her business anyway. "Dinner was a treat. Cal is now Olivia's new best friend. Or, maybe he's in second place to Theodore."

"Theodore? Who's that?"

"Ha. You'll have to ask Cal." Hannah didn't have to share everything either. She reached down to stroke Nellie's soft fur. Nellie leaned all her weight against Hannah's legs.

"Actually, I'm worried about Noah," Jack said, more to himself than to Hannah. "I know he and his buddies were hanging around those cottages after Caroline died." He rubbed his forehead. "What was his medallion doing in the sand? I saw him the day before Vern was shot, and Noah had it around his neck then."

"Have you told Pam?"

"I don't want to tell her. She already worries way too much about that kid."

"They might have stopped by but it doesn't mean he killed Vern. What would his motive be?"

Jack stood up and walked to his window. "I don't know, but it could be connected to that girlfriend of his. Tasha did not get along with her stepdad."

"I've only been here for a couple of days, but all I've heard is that no one cared much for Vern Mason. That doesn't help to narrow the field of suspects down much." Hannah joined Jack at the window. A car drove by and pulled into Hannah's driveway.

"Looks like you've got company. Want me to walk over with you?" he asked, concern lacing his voice.

Hannah had her hand on the doorknob. "No thanks, but I'll have to leave Nellie here. That's Meg picking me up. I'm not sure what it's all about, but she told me she has some information about Vern."

"Don't let her take you to that awful Pub and Pool Hall."

Hannah ran out the door and jogged to Meg's car. She could see several scrapes on the passenger side and half the rear fender was missing. Too late to back out now, she thought, as she opened the door and slid in next to Meg.

"Your cottage is dark, I thought you weren't home." Hannah had trouble catching her breath. "Were you out jogging?" Meg asked.

Hannah laughed. "Jogging? No, walking is more my speed but I was at Jack's house when I saw you pull in." She buckled her seatbelt. "So, where are we going?"

"The Pub and Pool Hall. My brother owns it."

Hannah's stomach flopped. Great, there had to be something sketchy about this place if Jack warned her not to go. Sketchy with a possibility of information?

They rode in silence, Hannah tried to keep her bearings, but after several quick turns down unlit streets, she knew she wouldn't be able to find her way home if Meg abandoned her at the pub. She patted her jacket pocket, checking that her cell phone was still there, and with any luck, it was still charged.

Finally, Meg bumped into a parking lot and shut her car off. A low building, the neon lights flickering 'ub and Poo all' told her this was not the high end stop for the Hooks Harbor tourist crowd.

"Here we are. Don't let appearances turn you off. This is where all the locals hang out, and if it's information you want, it's where you'll find it. The good, the bad, and the ugly." Meg tucked her keys, phone and wallet into a small bag that she slung over her head to settle across her chest. "I like to keep my hands free. Just in case."

"In case of what?" Hannah couldn't help but ask. She felt like a fish out of water and she hadn't even set foot inside the hall yet. She knew she was going to stick out like a sore thumb in this joint.

Meg grabbed Hannah's arm. "Come on. No time to be shy. They'll eat you alive if you don't get your 'don't mess with me' expression on. Caroline could fool anyone with her look." Meg watched Hannah. "Let me see what you've got."

Hannah took a deep breath, straightened her shoulders, clenched her teeth, and glared at Meg.

"Not bad but you might want to practice a bit to get it up to Caroline's level."

Meg pushed the door open. A rush of stale cigarette smoke, beer soaked wood floors, and buttery popcorn smells hit Hannah's nose. She coughed and felt her eyes burn. Meg leaned close to her ear. "You'll get used to it."

Meg kept her hand on Hannah's elbow, guiding her to the bar. "Hey Michael, found a new one."

Michael grabbed two mugs, filled them from the tap, and slid them down the counter to Meg, along with a bowl of popcorn. "Oh yeah? How'd you trick her into coming *here*?"

"I told her about your gourmet popcorn, right, Hannah?"

"Sure," she said, cool as a cucumber.

Michael's lip twisted up into an almost smile. After Hannah took a long sip of the draft beer and her eyes adjusted to the dim lighting, she focused on her surroundings. The click of pool balls came from the right side of the hall where all the action at the moment seemed to be centered.

After several minutes of listening to Meg and Michael chatting, Hannah asked Meg, "Is Michael your brother?"

They both laughed out loud. Michael leaned over the counter, putting his face next to Meg's, and asked Hannah, "Really? You need to ask?"

"Twins? You didn't tell me that before."

Meg finished her beer. "Didn't want to overload you with too much information. How about a friendly game of pool?"

Hannah nodded. The beer helped to relax her and give her the confidence she lacked when they first walked in. And, she knew no one at the Pub and Pool Hall was aware of her pool talent. But they were about to find out.

Meg introduced Hannah to the locals lounging around the pool table. Herb and Kirk nodded at Hannah between shots, pretending that the eight ball was way more interesting than the new girl at the pool table. Hannah analyzed her competition. Herb was, by far, the stronger player.

Hannah held her beer mug and leaned against the wall, not too far from Kirk as he waited for Herb to miss a shot. "New in town?" he asked.

"Obviously," Hannah answered. "I'm renovating Caroline's Café and Cottages."

He raised his eyebrows in surprise. "No kidding. You had to kill Vern to get him off the property?" he asked and laughed so hard he ended up with a coughing fit.

Meg winked at Hannah and asked the men around the table, "What do you boys know about Vern? He was always up to something."

Silence except for the click of the pool stick as Herb sunk the eight ball. Game over.

Kirk sighed. "It doesn't matter anymore, I guess. He was having some fun on the side, if you get my drift."

Meg handed a pool stick to Hannah, directing her question to Kirk. "Anyone from around here?" She racked up the balls.

Kirk shrugged. "I don't think so. He kept his dalliances private so Kelley wouldn't find out. That's why he rented the cottage from Caroline. He couldn't very well have his fling at their Inn, now could he?"

"You can break, Hannah." Meg pointed at the white ball with her stick.

Hannah chalked up her cue before shattering the triangle of balls. A solid ball rolled into the left corner pocket. With her focus on the game, she walked around the table, sinking three more solids before missing a bank shot. She had everyone's attention.

Meg moved into position, trying to find a clear shot at a striped ball. "You didn't leave me with much of anything, Hannah. Where'd you learn to play pool? I thought you were going to be an easy win for me."

Hannah let herself smile but remained quiet while Meg took her shot. She split two touching balls, sending a striped ball into a corner pocket and leaving the solid ball teetering on the edge of the opposite pocket. It rolled in, too.

Hannah cleared the table of solids and sunk the eight ball, before she hung the cue stick back on the wall.

"Nice game," a new voice said from behind her back. "It didn't take you long to find the local watering hole. Where's your sidekick?"

The hairs on her arm prickled as she turned around to see Chase staring at her. "How about a game in exchange for the rent Cal owes you?" Hannah asked.

"Nothing like a dame to rescue a prince charming in distress. And when I win? You sell your property to me?" Chase smirked.

Hannah kept her poker face in place, one thing she had perfected from playing cards with her father. That, and her pool talent. "I'll pass." She knew she couldn't wager something she couldn't deliver on, even though she had no expectations of losing the bet.

Chase laughed. "Just what I thought. All talk and no action." He racked up the balls and pointed his pool stick at Herb. "I guess you'll have to do instead."

Meg pulled Hannah back to the far end of the bar. "Be careful. Chase is the last person you want to be in debt to. You may be a good pool player but it's not worth it to risk being in Chase's clutches. Besides, Cal is a big boy and he can handle his own problems. Don't let his good looks fool you." She signaled to her brother for refills.

When Michael arrived at the end of the bar with the beers, Meg asked him, "What rumors have you heard around here about Vern having a girlfriend?"

"Only that he had at least one. Kelley was fit to be tied trying to get the scoop on what he was up to."

Hannah asked, "Angry enough to kill him?"

"Sure," Michael said, "but she was only one of many. What's your interest anyway?"

Meg said, "Hannah inherited Caroline's business. She doesn't want to end up like Vern."

Michael leaned close to Hannah. "Better watch your step. What I heard is that Caroline made a deal with Vern. She was pretty disappointed that you hadn't shown more interest in her and her business." He wiped the counter with a damp rag. "Whoever knocked Vern off has an agenda to get that property one way or another."

Chapter 11

Meg huddled closer to Hannah. "Why show up now and not when Caroline needed the help? Are you sure you're up to the challenge of taking over her business?" Her tone was challenging and gruff.

Hannah stared at Meg. She knew this question was a test and that she wanted Meg on her side. This no-nonsense woman had an inside track with the locals, she had been Caroline's right hand helper, and at this point, Meg was exactly who Hannah needed. But she had to play her cards just right to gain Meg's loyalty.

"My plan, and Caroline knew this, was to finish my education before moving here. Caroline was independent, not exactly a hidden quality. She never asked me for help." Hannah finished her beer. "I don't know what she said about me to everyone around here, but she never pressured me to come and help. I believe that Caroline thought everyone should figure out their own path, and she was a firm believer in a good education. Maybe only as a backup plan, but still, she valued my choice. And I had no idea she was leaving her business to me. Not until I got the call from her lawyer."

Meg slouched against the counter. "Well, I'll be. All along I assumed you were an ungrateful, spoiled, no good kid—just waiting for her to die so you could waltz in here and relax on the beach." Meg slapped Hannah on the back. "So, what's your next step?"

"I won't be selling, if that's what you're beating around the bush trying to figure out. I've heard the question, 'are you up to the challenge', at least three times in the last two days. Do you want to know the answer?"

Meg nodded, leaned back, crossed her arms and let her lips twitch up into a grin. "Can't wait. You're full of surprises."

"I don't know if I *am* ready or not, but there's only one way to find out. Sometimes you're faced with a fork in the road and I've decided to take it."

Meg's forehead wrinkled. "What's that supposed to mean?"

Hannah left a ten dollar bill on the table and slid off the bar stool. "Either path will lead me to something new and I'm staying in Hooks Harbor, taking the path to get Caroline's business back on its feet. Are you coming too?"

Meg took the money and stuffed it into Hannah's pocket. "I'm beginning to see a sparkle of Caroline in you. Of course I'm coming. I'm not going to miss this exciting ride." She slapped her hand on the bar. "Hey, Michael, tonight's on me. Add our drinks to my tab." Leaning close to Hannah's ear, she whispered, "He never makes me pay."

Michael waved to his sister as Meg and Hannah left the bar.

The crisp night air revived Hannah and cleansed most of the stale smoke from her lungs. "Interesting place, Meg."

"Interesting—such a safe word. Say what you really mean!"

"Okay," she raised one finger and counted off, "smelly, funky, dark, and dingy, with a touch of down to earth atmosphere." She glanced sideways at Meg. "How's that work for you?"

Meg laughed. "Much better. You nailed all the best qualities of the Pub and Pool Hall."

"No, I thought it was the *ub* and *Poo All.*" Hannah exaggerated the words. She was definitely feeling relaxed and was enjoying herself more than she probably should be.

"You crack me up. Just like Caroline used to. Boy, do I miss her, but," Meg bumped her hip into Hannah, "you're on your way to filling her shoes."

Meg dropped Hannah off at her cottage. When Hannah looked at Jack's house, a light was still shining through the edges of the curtains. Was he still up? She decided to walk over and knock softly. He'd either hear her or not. Hannah wanted to bring Nellie back to her cottage for company.

The quiet sound of conversation seeped through the front door. Hannah knocked. Nellie woofed. The conversation stopped and the door opened.

Jack's shoulders sagged but he invited Hannah in.

"I hope I didn't wake you up." She looked around to see who he had been talking to but discovered it was only the T.V. flickering silently.

"Can't sleep. Did you come for Nellie?"

"If you don't mind. I like the company, especially at night."

A slight grin formed at the edge of Jack's lips. "I knew she was the right dog for you. Do you want to sit for a few minutes? Tell me about your evening with Meg?"

Hannah made herself comfortable, suspecting Jack was the one who wanted to talk about what was on *his* mind, but she didn't pry. Instead, she entertained him with her visit to the ub and Poo all which actually got a laugh from him.

"I warned you about that place."

She nodded. "But I got some info about Vern having a girlfriend."

Jack waved that information off with a flick of his wrist. "Everyone knew that. He and Kelley were as good as divorced anyway."

Hannah leaned forward. "Did you know that's why he rented the cottage from

Caroline? That's where they would rendezvous."

"Odd. I never saw his car parked at the cottage." Jack jumped up. "There's another way in. It would involve a short walk, but a car, or even two, could easily be hidden from spying eyes."

"Just what I want to hear. Now I'll have to sleep with Caroline's shotgun under my pillow. Only problem is, Pam took the gun."

"Don't worry so much." Jack paced back and forth across his small living room. "Shall I walk you home?" he offered, revealing his own worries about Hannah's safety.

Hannah took the hint. Jack wasn't going to share anything but, at least, he provided a clue to why she never heard anyone drive to the cottage on her first night. That had been puzzling her. She never considered herself a sound sleeper but nothing disturbed that first night's sleep. The crashing waves lulled her to sleep better than any sleeping pill and Nellie never barked until the gunshot in the morning. She felt a tiny bit better knowing they both didn't sleep through the sound of a car driving right past her window. But dread also settled into her stomach knowing someone could sneak up on her unheard.

Nellie dashed through the open door, chasing shadows and boogeymen away before they made it the short distance to her cottage.

One more night before Cal would start gutting the place. It wasn't too late, she thought. She could get a head start on cleaning out Caroline's closets before climbing into her sleeping bag. It shouldn't take too long. With a living room-dining room-kitchen area, and a small bedroom, how much stuff could someone accumulate?

Two hours later, Hannah had the answer to *that* question. Some assorted clothes that would mostly be donated to the local women's shelter, a couple dozen books that Hannah would keep or recycle to her guests, and an old suitcase full of letters. The letters looked intriguing, but with her eyes getting heavy, Hannah decided they would have to wait for another day. She tucked that suitcase back inside the bedroom closet.

She climbed into her sleeping bag, patted the space next to her for Nellie to curl up on, closed her eyes, and was asleep in seconds.

The backup alarm of a truck jolted Hannah from a deep sleep. She shook her head, not sure where she even was for a couple of seconds. Not until Nellie woofed and ran to the door. A loud knocking got her moving fast. She tripped as she tried to step out of her sleeping bag, falling with a crash against a wooden chair.

"Are you all right in there, Hannah?"

"Hold on, I'm coming." At least no one was around to see that clumsy maneuver.

Cal held out a steaming cup. "I wasn't sure how you take your coffee, so I added a little cream but the sugar's on the side if you want any."

"Thanks. Cream and no sugar it is then." Her phone beeped with a text message. *Where are you? Thought you were picking us up at 8!* "Uh oh, I'm in trouble. I have to pick up Ruby and Olivia and I'm late. Want me to bring back some breakfast for you?" She looked around her cottage. "I won't be cooking anything here for a while."

"Sure. There's a diner in town. Okay food, well, adequate, decent prices. I'd recommend the breakfast burrito with extra salsa."

Hannah pulled her jacket on. "Sounds good to me. Okay if I leave Nellie here with you?"

Cal was already back at his truck, lowering the tailgate. "Sure. If she gets in the way, I'll call Jack to get her."

Hannah slammed the door of Ruby's rental car and headed into town. This was not a good way to start the day with Ruby. She was a person of strict routines and schedules, and being late didn't work for her. Hannah sighed. She had to find out exactly how long Ruby was planning to hang around.

News trucks and reporters clogged the driveway into the Paradise Inn. Hannah maneuvered her way past the crowd waiting outside the office door, finally finding a spot to park. Without thinking that she could be a target for the cameras, she wound her way through the crowd to the stairs to find Ruby.

Climbing two steps at a time, she rushed toward room number twenty, annoyed that Ruby wasn't waiting for her downstairs so they could escape the chaos quickly. A door opened, causing Hannah to jump sideways. Meg pushed a cleaning cart out to the hallway.

"What are you doing here?" Meg asked, pulling Hannah into the room she had just exited. "It's crazy downstairs and your sister is in the thick of it. Get her out of here before she makes trouble for you."

Hannah darted back downstairs, her eyes searching the crowd milling around. Sure enough, Ruby, with Olivia at her side, was smiling and chatting to one of the reporters.

"This can't be good," Hannah mumbled, just as Ruby's eyes looked into hers. "I better see what she's up to."

Meg grabbed Hannah's arm. "Wait. Don't let them know you're the new owner of Caroline's Cottages or you won't get a moment's peace."

"I'm afraid that ship may have already sailed." Hannah hurried away before Meg could ask for an explanation.

Olivia rushed to Hannah's side as soon as she made it to the bottom of the stairs. "Can we get breakfast now?" Olivia asked.

"You betcha, honey," Hannah answered and took Olivia's hand. "Let's get your mom."

Olivia skipped alongside Hannah. "Mommy has a new friend."

"Oh?"

"Yeah. I don't really like the lady. She didn't even say hello to me."

Ruby was walking toward Hannah with a newswomen at her side. "There you are, Hannah. I've been telling Missy Sharpe, all about how you found the body."

Hannah clenched her jaw, staring daggers at Ruby. "Is that so?" She tried to maneuver Ruby away from the reporter and get her moving in the direction of the rental car.

Missy held her hand out to Hannah. "Yes. So nice to meet you. And Ruby will be working with me on the exclusive story."

Hannah's jaw dropped. "What are you talking about?"

"My new job, Hannah," Ruby explained, her voice rising with excitement. "Missy called her boss at the Coastal Chronical news channel and told him she needed a personal assistant and, well," she shrugged and held her hands out, palms up, "one thing led to another and he said he would think about it."

Hannah looked at her watch. It was eight thirty. "You texted me at eight. All this happened in the last half hour?"

Missy put her hand on Ruby's back in a friendly but dominant way. "I'll let you two sort this out. See you," she checked her schedule on her phone, "at eleven? Does that work for you?"

"Perfect!" Ruby said as she basically pushed Hannah and Olivia toward the car.

Chapter 12

"Before you say anything, Hannah—"

"Say anything? No, you can't just waltz into my life and take over like you always do." Hannah's hand flew to cover her mouth. She was beyond furious but also angry at herself for lashing out at her sister.

Olivia looked up at Hannah with her big brown eyes. "Why are you two arguing? I want you to get along so we can live near you."

All the built up anger inside Hannah melted with that comment. Hannah picked Olivia up and hugged her. "Your right," Hannah glanced over the top of Olivia's head to look at Ruby. "We can figure this out like big people."

Ruby let out a sigh. "I need this job. I've got nothing. And if I live near you, it's a win-win for Olivia. Right?"

Hannah nodded.

“Ready for breakfast?” Ruby held her hand out for the car keys. “My treat.”

“I’ll treat today since I offered to pick up something for Cal, too. You can treat after you get your first paycheck. Okay?” Hannah held her breath, hoping Ruby wouldn’t be insulted. She suspected Ruby didn’t have much money, and getting into credit card debt, again, wouldn’t help Ruby or Olivia. Or Hannah, for that matter, since she would be the one to bail her out.

“Alright, but I will hold you to that.” Ruby slid behind the wheel. “Which way?”

They parked in front of Shipwreck Diner, chatting around the looming conflict of Ruby’s employment while they waited for breakfast burritos to go.

On the way back to Hannah’s cottage, Ruby asked, “Can Olivia stay with you while I have my meeting?”

Of course Hannah wanted to spend time with Olivia but, at the moment, she had a million and one things on her plate.

Ruby hastily added while looking in the rearview mirror, “You won’t be any trouble, right, sweetie?”

Hannah knew when she’d met her match. Ruby always could manipulate situations to make it work for her. It was impossible for Hannah to ignore Olivia’s innocent and hopeful eyes. She turned her head to look at Olivia in the back seat. “You can help me with Nellie. How does that sound?”

Olivia nodded her head vigorously. “And can we visit Cal on his boat? And Theodore?”

“Cal is working on my cottage today. Maybe when he takes a break, you can ask him about Theodore.”

Ruby remembered how to get back to the cottage without any help from Hannah. “I’ll drop you two off and head back to the Inn to get ready for my meeting." She blew a kiss to Olivia. "Wish me luck, Hannah. This could be my big chance to get my dream job as a T.V. reporter's personal assistant. The story about the murder is airing later today."

Hannah faked a smile, knowing Ruby was too involved in her own moment to notice. Poor Ruby, she always got her hopes up so high only to be disappointed time after time. Maybe this would be different, but Hannah had a sinking feeling that Ruby was headed into more than she could handle.

"Ready for a break?" Hannah called to Cal and held up the bag of food. She took in the sight of his lean body, carpenter belt, tousled hair, and dust speckled clothes. She could get used to this view, she thought, as her lips lifted into a half-smile.

He unbuckled his carpenter belt and tossed it onto the tailgate of his truck. "I see you brought another helper." Cal beamed at

Olivia. "And some nourishment. How about we sit and enjoy the view while we eat."

Olivia was already off after Nellie. Hannah and Cal made themselves comfortable and dug into the burritos.

After wolfing down half of his breakfast, Cal asked, "What's going on with Ruby? She seemed to be in a big rush to get somewhere."

Hannah shook her head and rolled her eyes. "You noticed?" She ate in silence, not sure what she wanted to share with Cal. She peeked at him from the corner of her eyes. He was relaxed, watching Olivia. It would be nice to have someone to unload on.

"I'm not too happy with her at the moment." Hannah finally broke the silence.

Cal lifted an eyebrow. "Oh?"

"She's talking to someone named Missy Sharpe from the Coastal Chronicle T.V. show. Have you heard of her?"

"Talking about what? That woman is a shark, always after blood to boost her career up the ladder. There's nothing wrong with trying to get ahead, but Missy, well, she'll use anyone and anything to get what she wants."

Hannah finished her burrito and wiped her mouth with her sleeve. "I forgot to get some napkins, want me to look inside for some?" She started to push herself up off the chair.

Cal's hand shot out to stop her. "Are you kidding? Look at me?" He pointed to various stains on his clothes. "Paint, grease, pine pitch, I don't even know what this is." He looked closer at the stain. "I think it's blood. Must be when I cut myself this morning. Believe me, I can live without a napkin. But thanks for offering."

Olivia climbed into the chair next to Cal, and Nellie flopped in the sand at her feet. "I'm hungry," she announced.

Hannah handed the last burrito to Olivia. "Try not to make a big mess."

"You haven't filled me in on your sister," Cal said.

Olivia piped up. "Mommy has a job offer. I didn't like the lady she was talking to very much but," Olivia shrugged, "I hope she gets the job so we can stay here with you and Hannah. And Nellie," she quickly added.

Cal's brows drew together. "A job?"

"Yeah, Ruby has worked with reporters in the past. I think she shared a bit too much with Missy, in her zeal for impressing her and hoping for a job."

Before Cal had a chance to respond, a shout interrupted their conversation. "Cal, hurry."

Cal jumped from his chair and rushed toward cottage number four with Hannah following behind. Monica's wheelchair was tilting sideways, one wheel sinking into the soft sand.

"What are you doing riding over here by yourself? Why didn't you call me?" Cal heaved the wheelchair backward onto firmer ground.

"I did call," Monica said. "Why didn't you answer?" She glared in Hannah's direction, clearly blaming her for monopolizing Cal's time.

Cal patted his empty back pocket. "My phone must have slipped out. It's probably in my truck. Sorry about that. Did you come along the beach?"

"No. There's a path from the road through those trees. I've used it before." She pointed to a barely visible opening through some scrubby bushes in the general direction of the road that led to her beach house.

Cal stared at the opening. "I never noticed that before. That could explain how Vern came the night he was murdered. And others could have snuck in, too."

Monica poked Cal's leg. "Don't be so dramatic. You're sounding exactly like that annoying reporter that showed up at my house this morning. That's what I want to talk to you about."

"Missy Sharpe?"

"Yes. How did you know she's in town? Has she been over here, too?"

"No. Not yet, but I have a bad feeling that it won't be long." Cal pushed the wheelchair closer to Hannah's cottage. "What did she want from you?"

"She wanted to know where I was and if I heard a gunshot. She knew details that aren't even in the paper yet. Officer Pam Larson shouldn't be blabbing to reporters."

Cal ignored that comment. Especially since Officer Larson had just parked next to his truck. Hannah left Cal to help his sister and she returned to see what Pam wanted.

Pam, with her hands on her hips, yelled at Hannah. "Did you tell that awful reporter that the murderer lost a gold chain and medallion in the sand?"

"Noah's medallion?" Hannah asked, trying to buy some time to figure out how to answer the actual question.

"Who described it as the *murderer's* medallion? Who made up *that* detail, Ms. Holiday?"

Hannah blinked. She felt her face flush. What had Ruby said about the gold chain Olivia found in the sand? No one mentioned that it could belong to the murderer, or did the reporter add in those details? Hannah's stomach clenched in a knot. Ruby was desperate for this job and it was within every possibility that she embellished the story.

"I don't know what you're talking about. I haven't talked to any reporter," Hannah finally answered, trying to keep her voice from shaking.

Pam pointed her finger in Hannah's face. "Believe me, I'll get to the bottom of this. Are you trying to divert attention away from the murder weapon? With your fingerprints on it?" She looked at Cal and Monica, listening in the background. "What are you two staring at?" Pam approached Monica. "What about you? Where were *you* early Friday morning? Riding around in your wheelchair, up to no good?"

Cal stepped between Pam and Monica. "Now wait a minute. You can't start accusing everyone of being the murderer. What facts do you have?"

Pam's mouth curved into a smirk. "Seeing your sister here made me realize she could have made it through the woods unseen. Who would suspect *poor* Monica? Stuck in a wheelchair. How long have you had that beach wheelchair, Monica? Everyone knows you'd do anything to help your precious Cal get the money Vern owes him."

"That's ridiculous, and you know it," Cal said. "How can Vern pay me if he's dead?"

Pam laughed. "You must think I'm stupid. Kelley's quite the rich widow now, isn't she? As a matter of fact, she's cleaning up all of Vern's unpaid debts. And that means you'll be getting a nice big chunk of money." Pam started to turn toward her car, then stopped. "I'll be watching all of you." She finally got in her car and drove off, leaving a cloud of dust behind her.

"Pam always had a chip on her shoulders," Monica said to the disappearing car. "Now, as a police officer, she has some power and she thinks she can intimidate all of us."

Hannah brushed a few stray hairs away from her face. She had a sinking feeling in her stomach. "I think it's more than that. Pam came here because she was upset about the information the reporter has about the gold chain. I suspect she's afraid Noah is involved in the murder and she's searching for any other possible explanation. Someone else to blame. I wouldn't want to be in her shoes—suspecting your own son of murderer."

Chapter 13

Cal helped Monica return to the path through the bushes, much to her annoyance.

"I'm not helpless," she scolded Cal. "The whole reason you talked me into this new wheelchair was to give me some independence. Now, get back to work."

Cal ignored her scolding. "Come on, Hannah. You should check out this path, too. If this is how people are sneaking onto your property, you should know what you're up against."

Monica mumbled between her clenched teeth, "If you weren't working here, you wouldn't be treating me like a baby.

Hannah and Olivia tagged along behind Cal on the well-worn path. Nellie darted every which way, checking out all the smells. She pushed through some thick undergrowth, returning with a crumpled bag.

"Give me that." Hannah crouched down with her hand out. Nellie abandoned the bag to rush after the squeak of a chipmunk.

Smoothing out the bag, Hannah read *Simply Sweets* on it. She tucked it into her pocket and jogged to catch up to Cal. Anyone could have dropped it, she told herself. Would the murderer be that careless to leave such incriminating evidence behind? She walked slowly, looking for anything else out of place.

Monica's wheelchair was on a track in the path that accommodated the wheels perfectly. "I'm all set," she told Cal. "Get back to your work. You don't want to disappoint your client."

"I'll stop by after work for a visit," Cal said, choosing to ignore her rudeness.

Hannah was behind them, but not out of earshot. Monica didn't like her, that much was more than clear. She whistled for Nellie and they turned around. When she got back to the spot where Nellie found the Simply Sweets bag, Hannah noticed from that angle, she could see her cottages. By tilting her head back and forth, she could see all the cottages to some degree, but the view was clear right into the window of cottage number four. And, the spot where she had left her gun was also clearly visible. A chill ran up her spine. Who was spying on the cottages? And why?

Cal caught up with her. "Sorry about my sister. She seems to have a bug up her butt lately."

"Her new wheelchair gives her more freedom. She must like that." Hannah hinted around the edges of what she was really thinking. Did Monica have a big enough hatred for Vern to spy on him? Or possibly murder him? She certainly had easy access to cottage number four.

"This path concerns me. You should think about some type of fence or barrier to stop that back door access. Especially in light of what happened to Vern. You never know who might be next."

Hannah stopped dead in her tracks. "What do you mean? Are you trying to scare me off my property?"

Cal's hand touched Hannah's shoulder. "Of course not. But it can't hurt to take extra precautions until this is resolved. If someone killed Vern to get him out of the way of buying this property, you could be in danger, too. That's all I'm saying."

"Or it could be something entirely different. Like a jealous wife or angry neighbor or blackmailing kids?"

His shoulders sagged. "It could be any of those things."

They continued in silence. Hannah was surprised that Cal didn't defend his sister. Was he thinking the same thing Hannah was thinking and what Pam voiced earlier? Who would suspect a wheelchair bound person?

Olivia broke free of Hannah's protective grasp when she saw her mother waiting outside Hannah's cottage. "Mommy!" she called.

Ruby crouched down to catch Olivia in her arms. The two twirled around and around, hair flying out behind them. Nellie joined in the excitement, jumping and barking.

"You look happy. Let me guess, you got the job?" Hannah asked.

"Yes. Yes. Yes. As soon as I get your permission for the broadcast to be filmed at the cottage where the guy was murdered." Ruby avoided Hannah's glare. "It's the perfect job." She set Olivia down. "Please, Hannah?" Ruby's eyes pleaded.

"No! I won't have that. This isn't fun and games. Someone was *murdered*," Hannah said with her voice lowered for Olivia's benefit. "And what did you tell your new friend about the gold chain Olivia found in the sand?"

"That it probably belonged to the murderer. What's wrong with that?"

Hannah moved right into Ruby's face. "You can't make up something like that. What if the person it belongs to hears that statement? And what if that person is innocent?"

Ruby's eyes widened. "You don't understand. I *need* this job." She glanced at Olivia. "I have to find a place to live and that takes money. I have to get Olivia back in school. She needs security."

"You should have thought about that before you got fired from your last job."

Ruby tugged on Hannah's arm, pulling her away from where Olivia was digging in the sand. "I didn't get fired. I had to leave. Olivia's father was getting closer to finding us."

"Ruby, when are you going to stop running? He doesn't even know Olivia is his daughter. At least that's what you've always told me."

"He doesn't, but I'm sure he can do the math if he finds me and sees Olivia." Ruby grabbed both of Hannah's arms. "Please. You have to help me."

"Listen. I can't stop them from doing the segment on a public road, but I won't let them on my property. That's where I'm drawing the line. And, Ruby?" Hannah waited to be sure Ruby was listening.

"Yes?"

"Don't make any more assumptions to get this reporter to like you. How do you know she's not just using you for her own gain?"

Ruby's head dropped down. "I thought of that, too, but I'm desperate."

"You and Olivia can stay in one of the cottages until you have an income and find a place to live. That way, I can keep an eye on her, too. Get her in school. A routine will be good for her. She can't just run wild on the beach with Nellie." Hannah let her mouth curve into a grin. "Something will work out, don't worry." She hugged her sister.

"Thanks," Ruby said as her lower lip quivered. "I'll take her with me to give you a break." She watched Cal pushing old appliances out of Hannah's cottage. "And give you time to get your cottage back into shape. We'll hang out at the Inn for a while and be back later."

After Ruby and Olivia left for the afternoon, Hannah left Cal to his work and she walked to Jack's house. Was Pam serious with all the accusations she made earlier? Sure, Hannah's fingerprints were on the murder weapon but she was never in cottage number four where Vern was murdered. She had to be careful. Being new in town, made it harder for her to know who she could trust.

Jack was behind his house filling his birdfeeders. Hannah hadn't noticed them before, but now she counted three hanging in various places around his yard. He had a big open wooden feeder filled with sunflower seeds, a tubular feeder with thistle seeds, and a wire basket with suet. As soon as he moved away, the birds flocked back to the filled feeders.

Nellie dashed toward the feeders, alerting Jack to Hannah's presence but barely disturbing the birds. "That's the main reason I wanted you to take her. She kept annoying the birds, almost as bad as a cat." He patted his leg. "Nellie! Come away from my birds."

Hannah laughed. "Nice try making yourself feel better about pawning Nellie off on me, but those birds couldn't care less about her."

His eyes twinkled. "Well, you are happy with her, and I knew that would be the case. To what do I owe the pleasure of your company?"

"Pam stopped by earlier."

Jack pressed his lips together. "She's dealing with a difficult situation at the moment." He pulled two chairs into a sunny spot in his yard. "Want to sit for a few minutes? My legs have been giving me some trouble lately."

"What kind of trouble?"

He waved his hand dismissively. "Just a muscle strain. I think I overdid it when I was cleaning my basement the other day."

Hannah settled into her chair. The birds were back in business taking turns at the feeders. "And what about Pam? She more or less accused me of being the murderer."

"She has to look at all the evidence, and the murder weapon is a logical place to start, even if, in this case, it's seems completely ridiculous to connect the murder to you."

"Yes, anyone could have taken the gun. I was stupid to leave it leaning against the cottage." She leaned forward, studying Jack's face closely. "What was Noah doing by the cottages the night before Vern was murdered?" She pulled the Simply Sweets chocolate shop bag from her pocket and showed it to Jack. "I found this not far from cottage number four."

"That's certainly not as bad as finding his gold chain in the sand." Jack rested against his hands, his elbows on his knees. "I don't know. I've been wracking my brain to come up with anything that makes sense. Sure, he and his buddies were using the cottages for parties. But murder? What would the motive be?"

"Could he have discovered what Vern was up to in the cottage and threatened to blackmail him?"

Jack shrugged. "I want to talk to him. Sometimes he opens up to me, and if he's in trouble, I'll see it in his actions. He's an open book with his emotions."

Jack stood up and walked toward his back door. "My phone's ringing. I'll be right back."

Hannah found a stick and threw it for Nellie. She dashed off, searching for the stick until a squirrel distracted her. Nellie barked and jumped on the tree where the squirrel sat safely above her on a branch, scolding the puppy with a constant chatter. Watching this gave Hannah a needed distraction from thinking about who might have been spying on cottage number four.

When Jack returned, his face was pinched and pale. "Pam just called. Noah is missing."

"Missing? Like, ran away?"

Jack nodded. "That's what Pam is afraid of."

All of Hannah's fears bubbled over with Jack's words—seeing kids on the beach the night before Vern was killed, finding Noah's gold chain, the bag from the chocolate shop, the path through the trees—everything pointed to Noah, and with his disappearance, Pam was put in a terrible situation.

A car door slammed in front of Jack's house.

Chapter 14

Hannah looked at Jack. Nellie woofed and ran to the front of the house.

"Dad? Where are you?" Pam called.

"Maybe I'd better leave. I'm not on your daughter's best friend list," Hannah said.

"That's ridiculous. Pam might not know it, but she needs a friend now more than ever."

Just as those words left Jack's mouth, Pam rounded the side of the house. Her long strides stopped and a scowl covered her face when she saw Hannah. "What are *you* doing here? Whenever there's trouble, you seem to be in the middle of it."

Hannah's eyes shifted from Pam to Jack, unsure of what she should do.

"Let's go inside and have some coffee, I know *I* can use some," Jack said, deflating the tension. Slightly.

Hannah and Nellie were the last to walk through the door. What was going through Pam's mind?

Pam slumped onto one of Jack's kitchen chairs with her arms resting on the table and her head bowed forward. "With Noah missing, I can't concentrate on the murder investigation. I have to find out why he ran away, make sure he's not involved in the murder." She mumbled more to herself than to Jack and Hannah.

Jack got the coffee brewing and rustled through his cupboards for something to eat. "Slim pickings here. Anyone want an oatmeal granola bar?" He put the box on the table, along with sugar and cream. "Help yourselves."

"Do you have any idea where Noah might be?" Hannah quietly asked Pam, feeling out whether Pam was ready to accept Hannah in the conversation.

Pam shook her head. She raised her head and her eyes only showed exhaustion. "He doesn't have much money, though, so he couldn't have gotten far."

"Do you think he's alone? What about his girlfriend?"

"Who? Tasha? Her mother keeps a close watch on that girl. She's always working at the chocolate shop or helping at the Inn."

Jack poured three mugs of coffee and sat between Pam and Hannah. He put his hand on Pam's arm. "I know you work incredibly hard which means Noah has a lot of unsupervised time."

Pam sat back, pulling her arm away from her father's hand. "What are you trying to say? You think I'm a bad mother?"

"No. You have a difficult job and you can't be in two places at the same time. This is hard for me to say, but considering the situation, we have to put all our cards on the table. Hannah saw some kids near the cottages the night before Vern was shot."

Pam shrugged. "Big deal. Kids were always using those cottages after Caroline died."

"Well, I thought it wasn't anything either. Until Hannah's niece found Noah's gold chain in the sand. I know he was wearing it the day before."

Pam stood up so fast her chair tipped over. "You think Noah's the murderer?" She paced across the kitchen, three long strides one way, then back again.

"Try to calm down. To answer your last question, no, I don't think he's a murderer but there are too many clues pointing to him being in the wrong place at the wrong time. Now, here's the important question, Pam. Was Noah home on Saturday morning?"

"You mean, did he have an alibi when Vern was shot?"

Jack nodded.

Hannah held her breath and squeezed her hands so tight her nails dug into her palms.

Pam sat down, her shoulders drooping. "I don't know. I wish I checked his room before I left for work around seven thirty, but I didn't. His car was in the driveway, but that doesn't mean he was home. He doesn't have an airtight alibi."

Jack opened a drawer and pulled out a pad of paper and a pen. "Here's what we're going to do." He slid the paper in front of Hannah. "Let's make a list of everything we know. If we're going to help Noah, we have to consider every possibility."

Pam chewed on her bottom lip. "I don't like having *her* hear all this information." She tilted her head in Hannah's direction.

Jack held Hannah's arm so she couldn't get out of her chair. "She's staying. Hannah has a lot at stake with Vern's murder. She doesn't need this cloud over the cottages, or her reputation, for that matter."

"Okay." Pam sighed. "Kelley has an alibi. She was at Simply Sweets with Tasha making chocolate whales and shells. So Tasha has an alibi, too. Cal and Chase were both on the beach around the time of the murder. Monica said she was at home." She looked at Hannah. "You were in your cottage, the closest to the crime scene, but no trace of you ever being inside cottage number four. Your fingerprints are on the murder weapon."

Hannah jotted down all the details before looking at Pam. "I discovered something interesting today. There's a trail on the edge of my property beyond cottage number four that goes through the trees to the road. It's how Monica got herself to my cottage in her wheelchair earlier today. There's a clear view of cottage number four from the trail." She paused. "And someone could have seen the gun leaning against my cottage, cottage number one. Anyone could have easily spied on the cottage, totally unseen. Maybe someone who knew Vern was using the cottage? Kept an eye on his activity and waited for the right moment to shoot him."

"Poor timing if you ask me. Why didn't they shoot him before you moved in?" Pam said.

Hannah shrugged. "No one knew I was moving in. It could have been a desperate move before they realized the cottages would be getting busy again. Or, whoever shot him didn't know I was there."

Jack nodded and pointed to Hannah. "Nothing looked different. You didn't come in a car. Vern and Chase argued with you that first night after you left my house. And they both saw the gun, but no one else knew you were staying in the cottage."

Hannah sipped her coffee. "So, does that give Chase an excuse for not being the murderer? He knew I was there?"

"Not really. He had a motive, he was on the beach, he knew the gun was there. I always suspected those two would come to some sort of problem over Caroline's land," Jack summarized.

Pam rubbed her chin. "This is all interesting, but it's not helping to find Noah. That's where my priority is now."

Jack carried the empty mugs to the sink. "You're right. You should go talk to Tasha. Did you know she has the same gold chain and medallion that Noah lost in the sand? I think those two were a lot closer than you realize."

"I saw Tasha wearing the medallion when I was in the shop yesterday. When I asked her about it, she tucked it inside her shirt. And I got the feeling she and her mom aren't particularly close," Hannah said. "Also, it was odd when I was in Simply Sweets. Kelley wanted to make me an offer on my property."

Pam stopped on her way to the door. "Too bad she has an alibi. Vern's death has made her a wealthy woman. And suspicion always falls on the spouse first."

Jack peeked out the window and Hannah heard the crunch of tires leaving Jack's driveway. "Good. She's got Noah to focus on and she's out of my hair. Now, we get to work."

Hannah's forehead puckered. "What kind of work, Jack?"

He sat at the table across from Hannah. "You know that shark Cal told you about?"

Her eyebrows raised even higher. "Missy Sharpe from the T.V. station? How do you know about that?"

Jack waved his hand dismissively. "Cal told me. But I have a plan. If you can't beat 'em, join 'em. Come on, let's go."

Hannah planted her feet firmly on Jack's linoleum floor. "I'm not going anywhere until you tell me about this plan of yours."

"We can walk and talk. You know, T.V. reporters love to interview local characters, especially an old guy who loves to share too much." Jack opened the door for Hannah and Nellie. "I figure I can beat this Missy busybody at her own game. And maybe it will help Ruby at the same time."

"Help my sister? You're talking in riddles."

Jack chuckled. "Not much gets by an old timer like me in this little town. Ruby doesn't want to be part of anything to do with Missy Busybody *Shark*. Of course, she doesn't know that yet, so I'm aiming to make all this work in our favor and not Missy's." They headed toward Hannah's cottage. "She won't know what hit her when she decided to come to Hooks Harbor."

“Why are you doing this? You barely know me and you know Ruby even less,” Hannah asked.

“Well, Caroline took care of me after my wife died. She refused to let me stay depressed and mope around. Instead, she challenged me to stay strong for Pam and Noah. I miss Caroline, but when I saw you standing in front of her cottage, well, it was almost like she was back. The way you looked me right in the eye and tossed your long braid over your shoulder was a flash of the young Caroline I met years ago. You didn’t have the luck to know her like I did, and that’s a shame, but you are as close to a clone of Caroline as anything I can imagine. By helping you, I’m paying back some of my debt to her.”

Jack looked away from Hannah but she couldn’t help but notice how he quickly wiped his cheek. A tear? Probably.

Hannah put her arm around Jack’s shoulder. No words were needed. They were a team, and right about now, she was happy to have someone watching out for her.

“Time to channel some of Caroline’s toughness. The media circus has arrived,” Jack whispered to Hannah.

Chapter 15

Hannah squared her shoulders and felt a surge of adrenaline make her fingertips tingle. This wasn't exactly what she would label as fun but it was exciting.

Ruby appeared at her side within seconds of spotting Hannah. "Can you keep an eye on Olivia for me? I'm not working but Missy wants me to observe her technique." She leaned close to Hannah. "You're not going to mess this opportunity up for me, are you?"

"I hope not. I think this drama has taken on a life of its own and I'm not sure what to expect," Hannah answered honestly. What she didn't say to Ruby was that she was keeping her fingers crossed that Jack knew what *he* was doing.

Missy snapped her fingers and signaled for Ruby to hustle over to her side. She handed

Ruby her coffee mug then pushed her off to the side like a piece of trash.

Hannah shook her head and bit her tongue. What she really wanted to do was walk up to Missy and shove her right into the ocean. Her mouth curved into a smirk at the image of Missy sputtering like a drowning rat with her perfectly coiffed bleached blond hairdo dripping salt water and seaweed. And the look on her face would be priceless.

The camera crew was done setting up and Missy, off to one side, was mumbling to herself, probably practicing her story and waiting for the live segment to begin.

Jack inched his way toward Missy, and before anyone noticed, he was standing next to her, whispering in her ear. She smiled and pulled him toward someone else. Missy's hand flew in every direction and her face held the excitement of someone who just won a multimillion dollar lottery ticket.

Ruby's eyes locked onto Hannah's. Her head dipped forward, then tilted toward Jack and Missy, sending a silent question to Hannah to explain what the heck was going on. Hannah shrugged, her forehead creased indicating ignorance of the situation.

They didn't have long to ponder what Jack was up to before a microphone was in front of his face and the cameraman had his lens focused on Jack and Missy.

With only the sound of the surf behind Jack's words, Hannah couldn't believe her ears.

"Well," he said into Missy's microphone, "I'm sure, without a shred of a doubt, that Caroline Holiday murdered Vern Mason. Yep, shot him right in the chest with her own shotgun."

"Mr. Jackson, Caroline Holiday is dead." Missy shot a glance in Hannah's direction. "Or, was that all some sort of fake death so the contract between Caroline and Vern was invalid and the property would instead go to her great niece, Hannah Holiday?"

Jack shrugged like a little boy. "Maybe so. She told me the contract to sell her property to Vern was no good if she died before the closing, and she did will her property to her great niece."

The crowd that was gathered around the filming crew gasped.

Hannah's eyes blinked and her mouth fell open.

Missy shoved Jack closer to the camera. "Tell us, when did you last see Caroline Holiday?"

"She came to visit me the night before Vern was murdered." He put his finger to his cheek and puckered his lips. "So, I guess that would have been two nights ago." He lowered his voice a tiny bit. "We have been very close." He winked at the camera. "If you get my drift."

Missy spoke into the microphone. "There you have it, folks. Caroline Holiday faked her own death and came back to kill her enemy, Vern Mason. What a clever plot. Who would suspect a dead woman of murder? You heard it first here, live on the Coastal Chronical."

The air was buzzing with the sound of everyone talking at once. Missy smirked into the camera as she babbled on about the town of Hooks Harbor and speculated on where Caroline Holiday could be hiding out.

The last thing Hannah heard was Missy suggesting that Caroline was staying right under everyone's noses in one of the cottages behind them. She turned and pointed at Hannah's cottage. "Look at all the work going on. Is there a secret room for her to hide in? Why haven't the police investigated this turn of events? Is everyone in this town conspiring to hide and protect a murderer? Let's see if we can get an answer from the," Missy put her fingers up in air quotes, "new owner."

Hannah tried to back away from the microphone that Missy pushed into her face. "What's your input on this exciting theory, Ms. Holiday? Did you actually see the body of Caroline Holiday to confirm she is truly dead?"

"I can't say I did, Ms.—what is your last name? I believe someone told me it's *Shark*?" Hannah asked with a flutter of her eyelashes, feigning innocence. Even if she didn't know Jack's plan, she could play along and add to the drama.

"It's Missy *Sharpe,* with a *P,* to clear up *that* misinformation." A muscle in her jaw twitched as she scrutinized Hannah with a piercing stare. "Mr. Jackson has certainly offered an interesting and clever new theory as to what happened," she pointed to Hannah's cottages, "right behind us and right under your nose. How convenient that you were sleeping a mere few hundred feet away from the murder but never saw anyone."

"You mean the ghost of my Great Aunt Caroline carrying her shotgun in a white gauzy nightgown?" Hannah floated her arms around in a ghostly manner.

"No. I mean Caroline Holiday, alive and kicking and out for revenge."

Hannah opened her mouth to throw another zinger at Missy but she moved away from Hannah, obviously loving having the spotlight on her and not wanting to risk another unexpected attack of sarcasm from Hannah.

Jack cozied up to Missy and smiled from ear to ear. He looked everywhere but at Hannah until Missy pushed him away from the camera. She walked off to the side with a self-satisfied grin. Then he winked at Hannah and followed Missy.

What now? Hannah wondered. She felt someone tap her shoulder.

“What is Jack doing?” Cal bent down and whispered in her ear. “Has he lost his mind?”

“He has a plan. I don’t quite understand it yet, but one thing I’m sure of, it’s going to get a lot of attention.”

Hannah finally looked at Ruby who was glued to her spot, her mouth hanging open and her face pale as the ocean foam.

“I better do some damage control before Ruby dies from the shock she’s going through.” Hannah pulled Olivia along and maneuvered Ruby away from all the commotion.

“Close your mouth and smile, just in case anyone is watching us.” Hannah tucked a few stray hairs behind Ruby’s ear and whispered to her, “Don’t expect me to explain what’s going on because I don’t know, but we’re going to play along with Jack’s plan. With some luck, it will work out in your benefit.”

Ruby's eyes blinked three times. She closed her mouth and picked Olivia up. "And here I was, hoping *you* had a clue. Caroline is the murderer? Who came up with that cockamamie idea?"

Hannah laughed as if Ruby had just told her the funniest joke. "Your new friend Missy *Shark* took it hook, line, and sinker. My guess is, Jack is trying to make her look like a complete idiot on camera." Hannah took a quick glance in Missy's direction. "I think it's working."

To add more drama to the already bizarre experience, Officer Larson pulled up to the crowd of gawkers. With a flash of her badge, she forcefully encouraged the onlookers to move along and clear the street. The crowd dispersed, leaving only Missy and her crew.

Pam, with her 'don't mess with me' look on her face, approached Missy. "Time to pack up. You're trucks are blocking the street."

She lifted her arm to look at her watch. "Five minutes and I want you out of here."

Missy whined in Pam's face, "But we're waiting for Caroline Holiday to show up. I promised my viewers an exclusive."

"Four minutes."

"How about we move off to the side?"

"Three minutes."

Missy huffed and stomped off, rounding up her crew. They loaded up their equipment and drove off. Missy glared at Pam through the passenger window.

Pam, with her hand on her hips, stared at Hannah. "Are you going to tell me what's going on?"

"You got here just in time," Jack said, saving Hannah from Pam's glare. "For some crazy reason, that Missy character thinks Caroline Holiday is alive and she murdered Vern for revenge."

“Now, where would she come up with *that* ridiculous idea?” Pam tried, unsuccessfully, to keep her mouth from twisting into a grin. “Clever though, if it were true. Who would suspect a dead woman?”

Jack slapped his thigh. “That’s exactly what *she* said.” He started to walk off toward his house but stopped. “Oh, and Missy thinks Caroline might be making another appearance tonight. At my house. She thinks Caroline and I are in some sort of relationship.” Jack wiggled his eyebrows.

“That woman is dumber than a bag of rocks if she bit on that worm. Everyone knows that Caroline was one of the guys and wasn’t looking for romance.” Pam’s radio called her. “I’ll have to catch up with you later. Kelley Mason is at the police station filing a report about a theft at Simply Sweets.”

Jack smiled. “Come back when you can. Any news about Noah?”

Pam shook her head and drove off. Jack headed toward his house. “I’ll be back with some of my special coffee and we’ll wait for inspiration from Caroline.”

Chapter 16

"How about I show you what I've done in your cottage so far?" Cal asked, gesturing with his hand for Hannah, Ruby, and Olivia to go inside ahead of him.

"Can I stay out here with Nellie and build a sand castle?" Olivia asked her mother.

Ruby looked at the ocean. "I'll stay out here and keep an eye on her."

Hannah went inside, followed by Cal. The cottage was surprisingly clean but naked with the old kitchen appliances, sink, and counter ripped out.

"Not much to see," Hannah said as she surveyed her cottage.

"Actually, I want to ask you what's going on with Jack," Cal said. "I've never known him to fabricate such an outrageous story, or did you plant the idea?"

"Me? No! I'm as surprised as everyone else. He wants to stick it to Missy in a big way—revenge for Caroline he said."

"Oh, that old feud about Missy's report of Caroline serving food that caused food poisoning. He always suspected she poisoned herself to give Caroline a black eye." Cal shook his head. "Jack never forgets and I wouldn't want to be on his bad side. He's as patient as a cat at a mouse hole. What's his next step?"

"I'm not sure. I think he's hoping to bring Caroline back from the dead to threaten, or at least scare the living daylights out of Missy."

Olivia and Nellie dashed into the cottage with Ruby right behind. She held the door for Jack, who had his hands full.

"Do you have mugs in here someplace? For the coffee?" Jack asked as he set the coffee on the small round kitchen table alongside a paper bag.

Hannah opened a cupboard door and carried over five mugs. Olivia picked out the mug with a spouting whale and Ruby filled it with milk. Jack filled the other mugs with his delicious smelling secret blend of coffee and offered Olivia a cider donut from the bag.

"My friend makes these cider donuts and dropped a dozen off at my house earlier. I think she's trying to fatten me up." Jack laughed and patted his flat stomach. "She thinks I eat them all myself and can't figure out how I stay so slim and trim. I told her it's my nasty personality."

"Can I have two?" Olivia asked with her hand already in the bag.

Ruby gave her a look and shook her head. "No, honey. Finish your milk. We'll go into town and get some dinner as soon as I finish my coffee."

Jack put up his hand to stop Ruby. "Don't leave yet. You need to hear this. I invited our friendly reporter to visit tonight so she can meet Caroline in person."

Ruby twisted around to stare at Jack, sloshing coffee down the front of her shirt. "You're officially off your rocker and I'll never get a job now."

Jack held his hands up, palms facing Ruby. "Calm down. Didn't you see how giddy Missy was when she talked about Caroline being alive and being Vern's murderer? I got her hooked and, now, we just have to convince her that Caroline is out to get her next."

Ruby's eyes narrowed. "Why?"

"Revenge. You and Hannah wouldn't know this, but Missy bashed Caroline's clam chowder last summer with a false accusation about food poisoning. Business tanked for a few weeks. I think she was hoping to drive Caroline out of business. Now she wants to shut Hannah down before she even gets started. She has an agenda with that property. I don't know what it is, but she's up to something."

Ruby set her coffee mug down. "I did think it was odd that Missy was so eager for me to be her right hand man. Now I'm starting to see the bigger picture."

"I'm relieved to hear that," Jack said, wiping his brow for dramatic effect.

Ruby worked, unsuccessfully, to mop the spilled coffee off her white shirt. "This is ruined. Oh well." She abandoned her task. "I have some news, too. This morning, when I arrived for my meeting with Missy at the Paradise Inn, she was in a huddle with Kelley. They had a map out on Kelley's desk. At the time, I didn't pay too much attention, but thinking back, I'm sure it was a map of the ocean frontage in Hooks Harbor."

Jack paced across his living room. "Can you get that map? It might be the key to what those two are cooking up."

A loud knock on Jack's door made everyone turn.

"Maybe it's Caroline," Hannah joked. "But she probably wouldn't bother knocking—she'd simply walk through the door."

Hannah opened the door to find Meg with her hand raised, about to knock again. "What took you so long? I need to talk to Jack. When I didn't find him at his house, I thought this place might be worth a look see." She walked past Hannah without waiting for an invitation and stopped abruptly when she finally noticed the others in the room. "What's this? Some kind of conspiracy?"

Jack pushed the door closed behind Meg. "You could say that. We're waiting for Caroline to show up; thought you were her."

"I've wondered when you would completely lose it." She stood with her arms folded across her chest. "Well? Who's going to fill me in?"

Hannah explained what Jack told Missy and that Missy now seemed to believe Caroline was alive and was the murderer.

Meg stared for several seconds before bursting into uncontrollable laughter. After gasping for air she managed to say, "Too bad Caroline isn't alive to hear this. She'd love it. Any more coffee in that carafe for me?" She helped herself to a cider donut while Hannah found another mug and filled it for Meg.

Meg looked around the cottage. "Are you fixing the place up for when Caroline comes back?" She chuckled and sat down, sighing as if the weight of the world was finally off her feet. "I have some information." She sipped the delicious brew. "I overheard Kelley yelling on the phone. I think she was talking to someone at the police station." Meg leaned forward. "She said someone robbed the cash from her safe at Simply

Sweets." Meg pursed her lips and looked at Jack. "She said the thief was Noah."

"Noah?" Jack fumed. "I can't believe it. How would he know the combination to her safe?"

"Why does Kelley think it was Noah?" Cal snorted. "Her daughter probably stole the money. Kelley always blames someone else and protects Tasha."

Meg finished her donut and took a swallow of coffee. "Kelley's been trying to break those two kids apart ever since I started working for her. Maybe even longer. The more she badmouths Noah, the more she pushes Tasha right into his arms. They spend as much time together as possible and I noticed they wear the same necklaces. Tasha told me she misplaced hers and asked if I'd seen it at the Inn's front desk."

"When was that?" Hannah asked.

"Saturday morning I think. Anyway, she must have found it because she's wearing it again."

Ruby pulled her jacket on. "I promised Olivia we'd take a look at the shops in town. Need anything?"

"Surprise me," Hannah said. "And don't forget your mission at the Inn."

After Ruby and Olivia left, Meg raised an eyebrow and asked. "Mission at the Inn? You people have too many secrets."

"Maybe you know something about this," Hannah said. "Ruby saw Kelley and Missy studying a map of the Hooks Harbor waterfront. Are they up to some plan?"

"It wouldn't surprise me, but I don't know anything. I'll ask my brother if he's heard something buzzing around the Pub and Pool Hall."

Cal wheeled Hannah's new appliances into the cottage. "You all can keep talking but

I'm getting back to work so Hannah has a place to entertain Caroline when she returns from the dead."

Jack grinned. "You know something? I hope Caroline is listening to our conversation because she'd be loving it to know she's still such a big part of our lives. As much as I miss her, I have to say, at least she brought Hannah to us."

Hannah felt her face heat up. "Thanks. I wasn't sure if I'd get much of a welcome two days ago with my arrival in town. When I had to threaten Vern and Chase with Caroline's shotgun on my first day, I wasn't sure I'd make it. And then finding Vern's body in cottage number four." She shook her head. "Ever since I discovered Caroline's suitcase full of old letters, which I haven't had time to read yet, I feel like she's been watching over me."

"A suitcase full of letters?" Jack asked, his voice full of anticipation. "That's a sign. Who knows what you'll find inside, but I wasn't far off when I said she returned. Let's have a look around cottage number four and see if there's anything the police overlooked."

"Finally," Cal joked as they headed out the door. "I thought you'd never leave me in peace and quiet."

Hannah walked between Jack and Meg. She pointed beyond the cottage. "There's the path I discovered. Let's take a look before we go into the cottage."

"These are strange tracks in the sand," Meg said, squatting down and measuring the width of the track with her hand.

"Monica used this path with her beach wheelchair. The path goes through these scrubby trees to the road and then it's not far to her house," Hannah explained.

"I wonder why she came over here," Jack said. "Monica and Caroline weren't exactly drinking buddies. I didn't want to bring it up in front of Cal, but when Pam suggested

Monica could be the murderer, it made me pause." He looked at Hannah and Meg. "It *is* possible. Vern is the reason Monica is in a wheelchair. He ran a red light, never slowed down."

"Wow." Hannah puckered her mouth. "That *is* interesting, and another layer to peel away in the murder."

Hannah couldn't help but wonder if Cal was protecting Monica or vice versa.

With Jack dawdling behind Hannah and Meg, looking at the best viewing spot to see the cottages, Meg broke the silence. "I quit my job at the Paradise Inn. Well, Kelley was probably going to get rid of me anyway, so I decided to beat her to it."

"Why would she let you go?"

"Vern hired me after Caroline died and, well, Kelley and I never got along." She shrugged. "With Vern dead, Kelley has big plans for the Inn and I don't fit into those plans. I don't mince my words and she doesn't want anyone disagreeing with her decisions. Are you planning to hire anyone?"

"I will need help." Hannah hesitated. Should she hire someone already when she didn't even have an income?

Meg continued, "Not right now, of course. I can survive for a few months. But if I know I have something when you're ready, I can relax a little."

"That sounds perfect to me. I don't know *what* I don't know about running this business! And with your expertise, hopefully we can make Caroline proud."

Meg slapped Hannah on the back. "I like your spunk. Caroline sure did make the right choice leaving this place to you. You've got her spirit and determination."

"I'm not sure about that, but I will give it my best shot, and thanks for the vote of confidence," Hannah said. "All I've been hearing for the past two days is—*are you up to this challenge*? That has made me more determined than anything." Hannah stopped in front of cottage number four, waiting for Jack to catch up. "Once Cal is done with the renovations and I have a chance to catch my breath, we can have a meeting and make a plan to be ready for a grand spring opening."

Meg hugged Hannah. "Thanks. I can't wait to get back to work here."

Hannah watched Meg head to her beat up car. If Caroline relied on Meg for all those years, that was good enough for Hannah. Besides, she told herself, what did she know about making clam chowder, crab salad, or fried haddock sandwiches? Hannah knew she could manage the financial part, but she definitely needed someone like Meg to help her learn the food part. Once she had time alone, she would look through Caroline's papers—in the office and Caroline's suitcase. With some luck, the recipes would turn up.

The sound of crunching sand broke Hannah from her thoughts.

"Ready to look inside?" Jack asked.

Hannah took the key from her pocket and attempted to insert it in the lock. She jiggled it, flipped it over, jiggled it some more, and finally got it to turn. "I better ask Cal to change these locks before this key refuses to work."

She pushed the door open. She sniffed the stale, cold air. An odd smell hit their noses. "What is that?" Hannah asked Jack. "Does it smell like garbage in here?"

"It sure does. Vern must not have cleaned the place up before he decided to get himself shot. Very rude of him, don't you think?"

"I'll clean it out before mice or rats are attracted." Hannah opened the cupboard door under the sink, looking for a trash container. "Here's the culprit." She pulled out a garbage bag overflowing with take-out containers, tuna fish cans, and every type of snack food package imaginable.

Jack peered over Hannah's shoulder. "Odd selection for someone who was fairly health conscious." He reached into the bag and pulled out an empty soda can. "I know Vern didn't drink soda. He was diabetic. Someone else was using this cottage."

A floorboard creaked. "Did you hear that?" Hannah grabbed onto Jack's arm and scooted behind him. "Or, maybe someone else is *still* using this cottage."

Jack moved quickly across the room and opened the bedroom door. "I thought it might be you in here."

Hannah held her breath. Who was Jack talking to?

Chapter 17

Her curiosity was stronger than her fear and Hannah inched behind Jack. She saw a boyishly handsome teenager— hands in his pockets, head bowed, and shoulders sagging.

Jack's voice softened. He put his hand on the small of Hannah's back and urged her forward. "Hannah, this is Noah. My grandson. You two haven't met yet."

Noah's eyes peered over his dark rimmed glasses. His mouth fell open as he raised his head. "You look like Caroline," he said in shock. "A younger Caroline," he clarified.

Hannah smiled. She didn't know what to say to this scared boy, but she wanted to know what he was doing in her cottage. The cottage where Vern's body was found.

"I can explain," Noah mumbled.

"We're all ears," Jack spoke for Hannah, too.

"When that reporter said the gold chain found in the sand belonged to the murderer, I freaked out and ran away."

"You didn't get too far," Jack said, relaxing his body and leaning on the door-jamb.

"Yeah. But who would look here? And besides, Tasha gave me the key. She's going to meet me later and she said she has a plan."

Jack sighed. "Let's sit down while you explain everything. But first, which one of you has a cell phone?"

"You can't call mom. She'll arrest me."

Hannah handed Jack her phone.

"I'll tell her you're safe. She's sick with worry." Jack dialed and had a brief conversation with Pam, insisting Noah was safe, uninjured, and Jack would take care of him. "No. I'll call you when he's ready to come home."

Jack dragged three chairs into the bedroom. "It might be safer to sit in here. You never know who might be watching this cottage from the trail." He pointed to a chair, and with a no nonsense voice, told Noah to sit in it.

Noah sat. He squeezed his hands together, twisting them in his lap. "Grandpa, I didn't kill that guy."

Jack's eyebrows rose. "I didn't ask you if you, did but it sounds like you have a guilty conscience. Do you know who *did* kill him?"

Noah glanced toward the window. He looked everywhere but at Jack or Hannah. "No."

Hannah sensed he was hiding something, or could he be protecting someone?

"What do you know? Hannah saw you on the beach the night before Vern was killed."

Hannah didn't bother to correct Jack. In hindsight, she realized it was Noah but she didn't know that at the time and only told Jack she saw some kids on the beach.

Noah's face paled. He looked at Hannah. "We saw you but it was creepy. We thought it was Caroline and that didn't make any sense. We were going to hang out here but Vern was using the cottage."

Jack crossed his legs. "Interesting. What was Vern using the cottage for?"

Noah squirmed in the chair. His face reddened. "Sometimes he met his girlfriend here. And then he told us to stay away."

Hannah leaned forward. "Let me get this straight. I know Vern had some kind of arrangement with Caroline to rent this cottage. How do you and your friends fit into that equation?"

Noah rolled his eyes. "Vern rented it for Tasha so she could get away from her mother and hang out with me. For some reason, Kelley doesn't like me and she wouldn't let me and Tasha hang out at her house. Vern was just trying to be nice."

"Yeah right," Jack mumbled. "Didn't it occur to you that sneaking around behind Tasha's mother and yours," Jack raised his eyebrows for emphasis, "was blatantly wrong on so many levels?"

"I just wanted to hang out with Tasha." He shrugged. "And Caroline didn't mind. She'd bring us food and let us watch movies here."

Jack paced across the room. "Who kept the key?"

"We hid it under the big shell on the side of the house. If the shell was upside down, we knew Vern was inside, but if it was upright, we could use the cottage."

"Hannah," Jack said so quickly that she startled. "Can Noah stay here for a bit longer until this mess is sorted out?"

Noah stood up. "I won't be here. As soon as Tasha comes, we're leaving together."

"That takes money, young man."

"Tasha's taking care of that."

Jack smacked the side of his head. "Did she steal it from her mother's shop? Because if she did, Kelley is blaming you for the theft."

"I didn't steal anything. Why would she say that?"

Jack put his hand on Noah's shoulder. "Listen to me. The world is not a nice place sometimes. You've lived in this little town your whole life. Nineteen years."

"Eighteen, almost nineteen to be exact," Noah interrupted.

"Okay, eighteen years. You have no idea what's out beyond these boundaries. You need family, a support system, not another teenager leading you down the wrong path."

Noah stood up. "You're just like all the other old people. Everyone except Caroline. She said to follow our dreams." He glared at Jack. "You can't stop me."

Hannah moved to the bedroom door. With her hand extended to show him the way out, she decided to call his bluff. "Go. If you think you've got all the answers, head right out this door. You're right, we can't stop you, but think about what's waiting for you outside this cottage before you rush headfirst into a disaster. Once everyone knows the medallion belongs to you, it puts you at the scene of a murder. You had access to the cottage, and you knew when Vern was here by the position of the shell. Kelley is accusing you of stealing from her shop. And—this is the most important detail—if you run away, it *makes* you look guilty." She sat down again, watching to see what Noah would do and hoping her instinct was sound.

Jack added, "You won't get far."

Noah hesitated. Before he made a move, yelling outside the cottage made all three of them jump.

Cal rushed into the cottage. “Hannah. Jack. My boat is on fire.”

Jack gestured for Hannah to go with Cal. “I’ll stay here with Noah.”

Hannah hurried out, zipping her jacket against the cold December wind. “What happened?”

Cal climbed into his truck and Hannah jumped into the passenger seat. “I don’t know yet. Monica called me. She heard it on her scanner.”

Jack’s knuckles were white. His jaw clenched. “I bet Chase is behind this. He’s been trying to get rid of me ever since I bought my boat.”

“If he didn’t want you there, why did he rent you a slip?”

"I bought the boat at the slip and the previous owner negotiated the deal without Chase knowing it was me moving in." Cal swung his truck into the Bayside Marina, parking off to one side away from the fire engines. "It doesn't look as bad as I expected. Maybe it won't be a complete loss."

The first person to spy Cal was Chase Fuller. A smirk adorned his face. "Well, well, well. Lookie what the cat dragged in. Too bad about your boat," Chase said with a voice that dripped of sarcasm.

Cal ignored Chase and headed toward the fire chief.

Chase's smirk disappeared when he turned to Hannah. "You've become awfully cozy with our town's carpenter. Watch out for that sister of his if you know what's good for you."

Chase started to walk away but Hannah's hand grabbed onto his coat. "What's that supposed to mean?"

"I guess Cal hasn't told you this part of his family history. Monica has had her eyes on your property since before Vern ever made an offer. She wants to tear the whole thing down to have more beach to herself. The settlement she got after her accident set her up with the money to do it, too." He scrutinized Hannah's face. "I hope you're ready to deal with her just down the beach from you, because the first time you step out of line, she'll be after you before you can blink."

"Monica doesn't intimidate me."

"That's what Caroline always said, too, but I think Monica wore her down. That's why she agreed to sell to Vern. Lucky for you Caroline died before the closing. Or maybe I should say, *unlucky*." His mouth twisted into a smile and he winked at Hannah. "Don't forget that I'm still interested. I'd kill for that property." As soon as the words left his mouth, Chase blanched. "Not literally, of course," he added, flustered.

"I'll be sure to keep that in mind. Especially the killing part," Hannah said to his retreating back.

"Are you okay?" Cal asked.

Hannah pressed her lips together. "Huh?" Her mind returned to Cal's problem. "Yeah. What did you find out about the fire?"

"The firemen already have it under control. I guess I'm lucky. It's just some cosmetic damage. And," he held Theodore up, "look who came out without one singed hair."

"He barely has any hair left *to* singe," she teased. "Olivia will be relieved. Who cares about the boat as long as Theodore made it out safe and in one piece?"

"Talking about safe and in one piece, what was Noah doing in cottage number four?"

"I think he's at the age where he knows so little, he thinks he knows everything," Hannah said. "His plan is to run away with Tasha. And you can't run away from the kind of mess he's right in the middle of."

Cal tilted his head and peered at Hannah. "What mess are you talking about? Is he involved with the murder?"

"He was nervous and evasive when we asked him questions. He knows something, probably a lot is my guess. And, most likely, Tasha was right there with him. He's not ready to share any details of what he knows or saw, yet, but his medallion didn't end up in the sand in front of my cottage by itself." The thought of what he might be involved in made Hannah shiver involuntarily.

The fire chief approached Cal. "We're all done. You were lucky someone noticed the smoke and called the fire in when they did or you'd be looking at nothing but a burned out hull."

"Did you figure out what caused the fire?"

"My best guess is a bad ignition switch. That would have caused all the smoke and, like I already said, we got here before it turned into a full blown raging fire." He slapped Cal on the back. "You won't be going anywhere with that boat anytime soon, Cal, but you can still live on it. That is, if you don't mind the smoke smell."

"Who called the fire in? I want to thank him," Cal asked.

The fire chief pointed to the office. "Chase Fuller. Lucky for him, too, because if the fire got out of control, it could have spread to the dock and other boats. I suppose that must be one of his biggest fears as the marina owner—fire, along with hurricanes."

The fire chief took one last look around before climbing into his SUV and leaving.

"I can't blame Chase after all. I suppose I have to swallow my pride and go talk to him. I never thought about what a fire would mean to the marina. Do you mind waiting?"

Hannah laughed. "I don't exactly have a choice. It's either wait for you to give me a ride back or start walking. No worries, I'll enjoy the scenery. I assume you won't be long."

"You're right about that."

Hannah meandered around the parking lot, noticing details she overlooked when she came for lunch and then dinner. There was a swimming pool, covered for the winter, surrounded by tables.

She walked slowly down the dock toward Cal's boat, reading the names on the stern of the other boats—Ocean Mist, Boat Bums, She Got the House, Freedom, Dream Boat. You could learn something about the owner from the name they chose, she thought. Cal's boat was named Seas the Day—nice play on words and the perfect advice for where she was in her life at the moment.

She was surprised to see very little damage, only some black near the steering wheel on the top.

Hannah felt a hand on the small of her back. "That was easier than I expected. Maybe I need to reassess my opinion of Chase. Give him a chance to show me he's not an idiot like I always assumed," Cal said.

"Seas the Day?" Hannah asked, pointing to the lettering on the back of Cal's boat.

Cal laughed a deep belly laugh. "Good one. Yeah, I should take my own advice. Holding a grudge against Chase isn't very healthy, especially since it's Monica's issue. For some reason, she doesn't like Chase so I thought I was being supportive by disliking him, too. I need to learn to let Monica fight her own battles." He guided Hannah back toward his truck. "Let's go and see how Jack is holding up with Noah."

Hannah was tired after all the drama of the last couple of days. What she was looking forward to was an hour or so to relax with a good book, then slip into her sleeping bag. But, of course, when she saw Pam's police cruiser parked in front of her cottage, she knew peace and quiet wasn't on the agenda for her evening.

Chapter 18

Jack was standing with Pam, his hands pointing one way, then another.

"I don't like the look of this scenario," Cal said to Hannah before they climbed out of his truck.

Pam immediately confronted Hannah. "You've been hiding my son here in one of your cottages? And it's the murder scene, no less?"

Hannah took a step away from Pam. "Listen. I didn't know he was hiding there until Jack and I went inside. He had a key that I knew nothing about."

Pam glared at her father. "You didn't tell me he had a key. What's that all about?"

Jack put his hand on Pam's arm. "I was only trying to protect you from information I didn't think was important."

She twisted away from Jack's touch and snarled between clenched teeth. "Let me decide what's important." She glared at her father. "Tell me everything. Now."

Jack told Pam about the shell where Vern hid the key and how Tasha and Noah were allowed to use the cottage.

Pam's mouth fell open. "I don't believe he would do something like that."

"Believe it or not, but that's what he told us. And after Hannah left, he told me a few more things." Jack stared at Pam. "You won't like this either."

She sucked in a deep breath and leaned against her car. "Go ahead. I need to know what I'm up against."

"Noah and Tasha planned to meet at cottage number four early Saturday morning since they couldn't use it Friday night."

"What time?" Pam asked.

"Early. Before Tasha had to help her mother at the candy shop."

"So, that sounds like well before Vern was shot."

"Maybe. Here's the thing," Jack said. "Noah didn't wake up, so he was late going to meet her."

Hannah could see Pam's tense muscles relax slightly. "He was home when I saw his car in the driveway. I wasn't sure about that," she said, her voice filled with relief.

Jack nodded. "Yes, it sounds like that's the case. But what about Tasha? Did she go to the cottage anyway?"

Pam slammed her hand on the hood of her car. "And why did he run away?" She turned toward her father again. "How could you let him slip out from under your nose like that?"

Hannah gaped. "Noah's gone? Weren't you with him?" she asked Jack.

"Don't *you* start on me, too. When I went outside to see what Nellie was barking at, Noah must have climbed out the bedroom window. By the time I realized he was gone, I called Pam and got a flashlight but there was no trace of him."

All eyes turned as a big SUV roared into the driveway and screeched to a halt.

"This can't be good," Cal said. "That's Kelley's car."

Kelley practically fell out of her car when she opened the door and the heel of her boot caught on her car mat.

Cal elbowed Hannah and she had to cover her mouth to hide her smirk. Nothing was funny about the situation with Noah, but the image of Kelley sprawled in the sand face first wouldn't upset any of them.

Once she recovered her dignity and smoothed her coat, Kelley pointed her finger at Pam. "Where is your son? My safe got cleaned out and now my daughter has vanished, too. And don't tell me you don't know anything about it."

Pam plastered an obviously fake smile on her face. "The only fingerprints found on your safe were yours and Tasha's. When is the last time you saw Tasha?"

"She was supposed to close up Simply Sweets for me since I've been overwhelmed with all the work at the Inn. After that, she was supposed to come to the Inn to help me get rooms ready for the big crowd coming in for the Clam Chowder Cook Off. Meg quit so I'm short-handed. How inconsiderate of her to leave me stranded when she knew perfectly well I'm swamped with work."

"Tasha?" Pam tried to steer Kelley back to the important issue.

"She never showed up. I would have come sooner, but I had to get all the beds made first."

"Of course," Jack said, his voice dripping with sarcasm. "Beds are *sooo* much more important than knowing the whereabouts of your daughter." His eyes burned with anger. "If you hadn't been so self-absorbed, maybe you could have stopped her from running off with Noah."

"Tasha would never do something like that. She knows I depend on her to be my right hand to keep these businesses afloat."

Hannah rolled her eyes. "Do you always blame someone else for your problems? I've only been here for a few days and the blame game seems to be your specialty."

Pam held up her hands to stop the arguing. "Listen. We have to figure out where those two kids could be going or hiding out. Any ideas?" She looked at Jack and Kelley.

Kelley puckered her lips. "I'll check Vern's house. They might think no one would look for them there." She climbed back into her SUV. "Call me if you find them," she hollered out the window before roaring away.

“No wonder Tasha ran off. With a mother like that, who needs enemies?” Hannah said.

Pam looked exhausted. “I’ll call around to other towns and put the word out that we’re looking for Tasha and Noah.” She hugged her dad. “Sorry to unload on you, this has been tough for me.”

“Don’t worry about it. I’ll call if I hear anything.”

After Pam drove off, Jack said, “Anyone hungry? We can eat and figure out a plan at my house.”

Hannah nodded vigorously. “I can’t remember when I ate last.”

“Well, I’ve got a surprise for you, then. How about you, Cal? Are you coming too?”

Cal hesitated. "I should clean up the mess at my boat . . . but what the heck, food sounds better."

As they walked toward Jack's house, Hannah asked, "Is Caroline cooking for us?"

"Ha! I don't want to ruin the surprise, but look at that car parked in front of my house. It looks like our friend Missy *Shark* arrived to wait for Caroline's arrival. I'll have to let her down easy."

They all burst out laughing.

Jack knocked on Missy's car window with Cal and Hannah watching behind him. Missy had been busy looking at her phone and she let out a tiny yelp. Her hand went to her chest.

"You startled me," she said through her half open window. "Am I too late?"

"I'm afraid so. Caroline called and said she wasn't feeling too well and wouldn't be stopping for a visit. She also asked me to tell you to watch your back. She hasn't forgotten what you did to her last summer." Jack leaned right up to the car window. "You might want to just skedaddle out of town. You know—for your own safety."

Missy's mouth fell open. "Are you threatening me, Mr. Jackson?"

"Me?" he said sounding totally innocent. "Of course not! I'm only passing on a message. Now, you take it any way you please, young lady. But if it was me, I don't think I'd want to hang around with *that* unknown making me watch over my shoulder all the time." He reached through the window and tapped Missy on her shoulder.

She let out another shriek and twisted her head around as if she suspected there was someone in the back seat of her car.

Hannah walked around the back of the car, followed by Cal. It was all they could do to keep from bursting into laughter. Missy's car tire spun in the sand before it shot away into the darkness.

Jack slapped his thigh. “Did you see her face? I sure gave her something to think about.”

“You certainly did,” Hannah managed to squeak out through each new snort of laughter. “And I wouldn’t be surprised if she wet herself when you tapped her shoulder.”

After they managed to pull themselves together, Jack commented, “The lights are on inside. Let’s see if the food is ready.”

“Who’s the mystery guest? Caroline?” Cal asked.

“Sort of,” Jack said.

That hint only made Hannah more curious. She knew it was preposterous, but could Caroline actually still be alive? From what everyone said about her, if anyone would fake their own death, she sounded like the perfect candidate. Hannah shook the thought away as she walked through the front door that Jack held open for her.

The most delicious seafood smell filled Jack's house. Clanging sounds, mixed with a bit of cursing, came from his kitchen.

"It's about time you got here. The clam chowder's starting to stick to the pot. If it's ruined, I'm blaming you, Jack."

"Calm down, Meg. You know it won't taste like Caroline's clam chowder unless there are little bits of potatoes that need to be scraped from the bottom of the pot. She always said that's what made it special."

"What have you been doing? You told me you'd be here," Meg checked the time, "an hour ago."

Hannah picked up the recipe on the counter. "This doesn't look complete." She flipped the paper over. "Potatoes, clams, half and half—where's the rest of the recipe?"

Meg grinned and tapped her head. "The rest is up here. Caroline didn't believe in following a recipe. She always said it was more like a guide and she would experiment until she got it right. That rubbed off on me too, I guess."

Jack sat at his kitchen table. "We're late because there was a bit of trouble at the cottages. Noah and Tasha have disappeared. Pam is putting the word out to other towns and Kelley is searching Vern's house."

Meg moved the pot of chowder off the burner and turned around. "Missing?"

Jack nodded.

Meg ladled soup into four bowls and Hannah carried them to the table. She went back to the counter for a box of crackers and spoons before sitting down.

Meg sat down, her finger on her lips. "I heard Tasha whispering on her phone when I went to the Inn to get my last check.

It didn't mean much at the time, but now I wonder if she was making plans with Noah."

Hannah blew on a spoonful of clam chowder. "What did you hear?" She slurped the chowder. "This is fantastic. You'll have to teach me how to make it," she said to Meg.

"I heard," she leaned her chin on her hand, "Tasha say something about sandwiches, water, and a boat."

"A boat? At this time of year?" Cal said, his face wrinkled in confusion.

"I know. I guess I should have paid closer attention but that's all I can remember," Meg replied.

They ate in silence except for the clink of spoons on the sides of the bowls and Nellie's nails clicking on the floor as she walked from one person to another, hoping for a handout. Jack must have trained her to beg already, Hannah thought.

Hannah couldn't help but wonder what Tasha and Noah were up to and why did they run away? What did they know about Vern's murder?

Cal and Hannah walked back toward her cottage. Nellie dashed after every shadow that flickered along their walk.

Hannah yawned.

"It's been a long day for you," Cal said.

"A bit of an understatement," she said and laughed. "I will admit that I can't wait to sink inside my sleeping bag."

"I'll be back early to finish up in your kitchen and get started on sanding the floors." He paused as they reached his truck. "I've been thinking about what Meg said she overheard Tasha saying on the phone."

Hannah tilted her head and raised her eyebrows.

"Tasha said something about a boat. I can't get that out of my mind," Cal told Hannah.

Chapter 19

Hannah let her body relax one muscle at a time inside her soft, down sleeping bag as she drifted toward sleep. Nellie curled up in her usual spot, leaning against Hannah's legs. Once Cal finished the renovations, she decided as she drifted toward sleep, she would give up her camping mentality and turn the cottage into a genuinely cozy living space. For now, she had no choice but to continue living out of her backpack.

Cal's truck door slamming shut woke Hannah from a dreamless sleep. She hopped up and pulled a warm fleece over her pink penguin flannel pj's. This was awkward and not exactly the image she wanted Cal to see. With the chilly nights, she had salvaged the warm flannels from Caroline's dresser.

Of course, by the time she opened the bedroom door, he was already in her main room with two coffees. That was considerate. I could get used to this, she thought, as the aroma made her brain buzz.

Cal's lips twitched at the corners. "Cute."

Hannah extended her arms to the sides and spun around, deciding she may as well own the image gracefully. "And speaking of cute, how did Theodore make out after the trauma he went through in your boat fire?"

"A kiss and a band aide and he's as good as new." Cal sipped his coffee. "Those jammies look familiar."

"Yeah, I found them in Caroline's dresser." Hannah shrugged and her eyes twinkled. "I hope she doesn't mind."

"The more I see you, the more of Caroline appears. With your looks, words, and now your clothes, maybe Jack is partially right—Caroline is still alive—in you."

With the mention of Jack's name, the door opened and he walked in carrying a bag. "Meg left these for me to share. She said they're much tastier fresh from the oven but they're still pretty delicious today. Help yourselves."

Hannah looked at her unfinished kitchen and was thankful that someone else was taking care of her stomach. She peeked inside the bag. "Oooh, my favorite! Cinnamon rolls."

Jack and Cal exchanged a look and laughed.

"What?" Hannah asked. "Why are you two laughing at me?"

"Cinnamon rolls were Caroline's favorite, too, and one of the sweets she had on the menu. And, she always had a plate in the office for the guests at the cottages to enjoy with a cup of coffee when they rolled out of bed."

"That sounds like a tradition to keep." Hannah took a big bite of the sticky sweetness and licked her fingers. "Have you heard anything from Pam? Or Noah?"

Jack shook his head. "Nothing yet."

Cal finished his coffee. "I talked to Chase this morning and asked him to keep an eye out for Noah and Tasha. Just in case they have a connection to someone's boat at his marina."

Jack lifted an eyebrow. "You and Chase? Since when do you two talk civilly to each other?"

"He's the reason my boat didn't burn up. He saw the smoke and got the fire department before the fire turned into a blazing inferno." Cal shrugged. "It's well past time to move beyond our differences."

"Be careful. I'm not sure you can ever trust him one hundred percent," Jack said.

Before Jack could explain that comment, the door opened.

"You all are up bright and early," Ruby greeted the crowd.

Nellie crashed into Olivia who fell in a laughing heap. Nellie seemed to be just as excited to see the little girl as Olivia was to see the puppy.

Ruby had her own mug of coffee and helped herself to the last cinnamon roll. “Where did these come from,” she asked between chews. “The best cinnamon roll I’ve ever had.”

“Meg makes them,” Jack said. “You’ll need to try one when they’re still warm from the oven.”

Ruby offered a bite to Olivia who shared it with Nellie.

“Well, that’s a waste. I would have eaten the whole thing if I knew you were going to waste it on the dog.” Ruby unsuccessfully looked for something to wipe her hands on. Instead, she had to resort to her own jeans. “Anyway,” she pulled a paper from her purse. “I found this.”

She unfolded the paper to reveal a map. Jack, Cal, and Hannah pounced on the paper.

"Where did you find it?" Jack asked, almost breathlessly.

Ruby coyly flicked her wrist. "I noticed Kelley leave her office in a big hurry. You know, it's chaos at the Inn. She's so shorthanded. I wouldn't be surprised if she has a nervous breakdown. Oh, of course she tries to hide it all under her phony veneer of 'I've got everything under control' look, but I can see right through that."

Hannah's heel tapped impatiently. "The map?

Ruby's eyes flashed annoyance that Hannah interrupted her. "I'm getting to that. Do you want the whole story or not?"

"Yeah, yeah. Spit it out." Hannah made a circular motion with her hand.

"Where was I? Oh yeah, the reason Kelley rushed out without closing her office door?" She raised her eyebrows and waited for everyone's undivided attention. "Pam arrived with a search warrant. I don't have a clue what she's looking for, but Kelley was in a complete panic."

Hannah looked at Jack. "Do you know anything about a search warrant?"

He shook his head. "The only thing I can imagine is that they want to look over the books for a possible motive, but that's speculation on my part."

"So, anyway," Ruby continued her story, "I took a quick detour into Kelley's office, and lo and behold, the map was sitting right on top." Ruby patted herself on the shoulder. "I did her a favor getting it out of there moments before Pam walked around the corner heading right to the office. Kelley was giving all kinds of excuses why Pam had no right to look through Vern's files."

Jack chuckled. "I bet that made a big impact."

"Oh, it did. Pam threatened to throw Kelley in jail if she didn't cooperate."

Hannah smoothed the map out on top of her new counter. "This doesn't mean a pile of clam shells to me. What's this X anyway?"

"Huh, it looks to be right under the café. See, here's my house, and that's Monica's house, and the X is right in the middle. If the X indicates something of value, it could explain why so many people were after this property," Jack concluded. "And why Caroline decided to fake her own death," he added with a twinkle in his eye.

"Stop that kind of talk," Ruby said. "Don't make fun of the dead. She was our great aunt after all." Ruby's eyes bored into Jack. "Do you know something about Caroline's death that we haven't been told?"

“Nope. I like the idea of her still being out and about somewhere. That’s all I’m saying.” He winked at Hannah.

Hannah folded the map. “We need to keep this someplace safe. Kelley will miss it eventually. Ruby, is Missy still hanging around the Inn?”

“She sure is, and she told me about the Clam Chowder Cook Off this afternoon. She’s super excited to be one of the judges this year. Now that Kelley became the last minute host of the event, Missy finally got asked. Apparently, Vern didn’t like her and wouldn’t let her be a judge. At least that’s what she told me.”

“I’ll safeguard this.” Jack tucked the map in the inside pocket of his jacket and patted it smooth. “Meg always wins the Clam Chowder Cook Off. And the day she loses? You won’t want to be around her.”

"Was Meg's chowder she made last night the recipe she enters in the competition?" Hannah asked.

"Probably. Somehow, it always tastes a bit different every year. And she always wins."

"What's the prize?"

"A clam shaped bowl. It's not the prize that counts, but it generates a lot of publicity for the winner, and in Meg's case, that publicity always helped Caroline's café," Cal explained. "At least until Missy wrote that article about getting food poisoning from Caroline's clam chowder."

Jack had a devilish grin on his face. "I think Missy may regret being a judge this year."

Hannah tilted her head. "Why is that? Do you know something?"

"What goes around comes around. I wasn't planning to go this year, but with everything Ruby just told us, I've changed my mind."

Cal slit the cardboard off the new stove. "You might want to move your coffee klatch to another location while I get back to work on Hannah's apartment. That is, if she cares to get this place finished anytime soon. With any luck, I'd like to have this kitchen done today."

Ruby said, "I'm going to head back to the Inn to keep an eye on the Clam Chowder Cook Off set up. Come on Olivia."

Jack put his cap on. "I have to go see a man about some clams."

"What's that all about?" Hannah asked Cal after Jack left.

"I'm not sure, but if I know anything about Jack, he has something up his sleeve. And I don't think it will be anything good for Missy Sharpe."

"Will he poison her bowl of chowder?" Hannah's eyes were as big as saucers.

"No, nothing that dramatic. And whatever his plan is, he'll blame it on Caroline. He's having way too much fun blaming everything on her."

Cal's phone beeped with a message. After reading it, he said to Hannah, "That was Chase. He has some information about Noah and Tasha. Can you go talk to him so I can keep working here?"

"Sure. Should I let Jack know?"

Cal scrunched up his lips. "No. Let's keep him out of the loop for now. Find out what Chase knows first. No point in getting his hopes up if it turns out to be nothing."

Hannah left Nellie with Cal and drove to the marina. The sun was bright, giving the false feeling of warmth, but as soon as she stepped out of her car the blustery wind took her breath away. She stuck her hands in her jacket pockets and pulled the fleece tight. It was going to take some time getting used to this coastal weather.

As she walked to the office door, various thoughts raced through her mind. Would Noah and Tasha be sitting inside? Or would Chase have grim news about them?

The small office was empty when she poked her head in, but the sound of the door alerted Chase to her presence.

"I'll be right out," he called from another room. He entered with an armful of papers. "Oh. I wasn't expecting *you*. Where's Cal?"

Hannah was a bit taken aback by his abrupt and unfriendly tone. "He asked me to come to find out what you know about Noah and Tasha."

Chase dumped the papers on his desk. He pointed to a chair. "Have a seat. Coffee?"

Hannah wondered how long the coffee had been sitting in the pot, but if it was warm, at least it would take the chill out of her hands. "Yes please."

Chase took two Styrofoam cups from the cupboard and poured the coffee. "I hope black is okay," he said as he handed Hannah a cup. "I just ran out of cream and sugar."

"Well, black it is then." She smiled and waited for Chase to sit down too.

He sipped his coffee. "This is awful. You won't hurt my feelings if you don't drink it." He set his cup on his desk and studied Hannah. "You brought quite the drama to our little town. Just like Caroline, always a whirlwind surrounding her."

"You know, I barely knew her."

"Really? You are the spitting image of a younger Caroline. The similarities are, well, a bit unnerving. And it certainly is odd that she would leave that valuable property to someone she barely knew." His eyes burned into Hannah.

She stared right back. "I would say it's odd that you don't have an alibi for the morning

Vern was shot. Why were you so keen to get that property?"

Chase laughed. "I didn't want Vern to have it." Chase sat back and laced his fingers together across his chest. "I appreciate the beauty of the beach, but Vern's plan was to tear down the small rustic cottages and build an eyesore of a motel or some other hideous structure. Your new friend Jack didn't want that either. And, like I told you yesterday, Cal's sister wants to get rid of the cottages, too, but at least she didn't have plans to rebuild anything."

"Who do you think killed Vern?"

He shrugged. "I don't know and I don't care. He's dead and his plans are done, unless there's some loophole in the contract and his wife can get the property away from you. You'd better watch out for Kelley. If there's a way to make the contract stick, she'll figure it out."

"Cal said you had some information about Noah and Tasha." Hannah wanted to get the information and leave. Something about Chase made her squirm.

"I seem to be bailing Cal out every time I turn around. He's going to owe me big time." Chase leaned forward. "I think those two kids stayed in one of the boats that are stored for the winter. I noticed the tarp was loose so I took a look inside and found some empty soda cans and an empty Simply Sweets bag."

"Maybe the owner never cleaned up the boat and left that stuff inside."

"I doubt it. The guy is a neat freak." Chase shrugged. "I told Cal I would let him know if I noticed anything and I'm a man of my word, so make sure you relay my message." He stood up. "And I'll give you some free advice—watch your back and be careful who you trust."

"Including you?"

Chase smirked. “Including me.”

Chapter 20

Hannah closed the office door behind her, happy to leave and be out of Chase's view. The guy oozed less than warm and friendly, more like if you turn your back he could freeze you with his stare.

As she headed back toward her cottage, she was surprised to see Monica riding down the edge of the road on her wheelchair and veer off onto the path that led to the back entrance to her cottages. She was moving that wheelchair along at a pretty good clip. What was *she* up to?

Hannah slowed down, parking in front of Jack's house instead of her own. It was time to find out more about Monica. Like Pam had said, who would suspect someone in a wheelchair of being able to get to the cottage and shoot Vern? And, Hannah decided Jack needed to know about his grandson, even if Cal wanted to keep him out of the loop.

Jack opened the door as soon as Hannah knocked and motioned for her to come inside as he talked to someone on his phone. All she heard was Jake saying he'd stop on his way to the Clam Chowder Cook Off.

"Come in. Come in," Jack said enthusiastically. "I don't have much time. I'm meeting my friend in," he checked his watch, "thirty minutes."

Hannah left her jacket on and followed Jack into his living room. "I had an interesting chat with Chase Fuller."

"Oh?" Jack said with a significant amount of surprise in his voice. "Did he show up to harass you about selling your land?"

"No. I went to the marina. He had some information about Noah and Tasha."

Jack's face went blank. His hand reached out to rest on the back of the couch for support. "And?" A new crease formed in his forehead.

"Chase thinks they snuck into one of the boats that is stored for the winter. Someone left soda cans and an empty Simply Sweets bag."

"Oh. Sounds like Noah's favorite drink, just like we found in cottage number four. I'd better let Pam know so she can keep an eye on the marina in case they go back."

"Wait." Hannah touched Jack's arm. "If the police are there, won't that spook the kids away? How about asking Cal?"

"Yeah, that's a good idea." Jack pulled his jacket off the back of the couch. "Let's go ask him."

"Before we go to my place, there's something else I want to ask you."

Jack slipped his arm into his jacket sleeve.

"On my way here, I saw Monica rushing down the street to the path to my cottages. She looked to be on a mission. What's her story? She wants my property, too?"

"Monica? What the devil would she do with *your* place?"

"Tear it down?"

"That sounds like poppycock. Who told you that rubbish?"

Hannah waved her hand dismissively. "Doesn't matter. But what about her accident? What happened?"

"I already told you. Vern ran the red light, t-boning her car on the driver side. She's lucky to be alive but she doesn't see it that way. He walked away with barely a scratch. She can't get past how the accident changed her life, and Cal's since he left medical school to help her."

"But she got a big financial settlement?"

"That's rubbish, although she got some money which is only fair. I don't know the exact details, but the settlement helped to pay for converting her house to be wheelchair accessible and it supplements her income. I've always suspected Chase Fuller to be behind the rumor that she got millions. I know that's what everyone says about her and, Monica being Monica, she never comments on the rumors. But believe me, she has to work like everyone else." Jack headed to his door, holding it open for Hannah. "Do you think Monica murdered Vern?" he asked.

"It *is* possible. Your daughter was the first one to say it. She has a huge motive, no alibi, and easy access to the murder scene. What do you think?"

"Possible for sure but I wouldn't be telling Cal your idea. He and Monica are like this." Jack held up his hand with his middle finger wrapped tightly around his index finger.

As they got closer to Hannah's cottage, Nellie dashed over to greet them. She danced around their legs until Hannah reached down to pat her.

Jack chuckled. "Go ahead, you can tell me I was right about you needing a dog."

Hannah tried to scowl and pretend Jack had it all wrong but her mouth betrayed her and broke into a big grin instead. "Yeah, you were right. I am happy to have her for company, especially after Vern was murdered. Between the two of us, we should hear any intruders."

Jack elbowed Hannah. "Speaking of intruders. When you saw Monica on the road earlier, she must have been hightailing it over to find Cal."

Cal and Monica were outside Hannah's cottage. Cal's head was bowed like he was getting a tongue lashing from Monica. The breeze carried the sound of their voices but the words were muffled until Hannah was only a car length away.

"If you don't do something about it, I will," Hannah heard Monica say before Cal glanced over her head and saw Hannah and Jack approaching.

The tension in Cal's face faded away as he smiled at Hannah "Monica has some news I think you'll be interested in hearing."

Monica turned her head and scowled when her eyes met Hannah's. "I'm just leaving." She turned her wheelchair and headed back to the path through the bushes.

"She saw Jack's grandson sneaking through the bushes to cottage number four early this morning."

"Was he alone?" Jack asked.

"She only saw one person."

Jack began to walk to the cottage. "I'll check if he's still there."

Cal held Hannah's arm, preventing her from following Jack. "The other thing is, Monica saw Noah running away from the cottage the morning Vern was killed. She thinks Noah is the murderer. She knows he used the cottage on a regular basis to meet up with Vern's stepdaughter."

"Really? Why hasn't she told that to the police?" Hannah said with skepticism filling her words. She left plenty unsaid—what was Monica doing spying on the cottage?

"Monica doesn't have any faith in Pam investigating her own son. She's afraid Pam thinks *she* shot Vern."

"So, now, several days later, she points the finger at someone else?" Hannah shook her head. "I'm no expert, but this sounds fishy to me. I know about the accident she had and that she never forgave Vern. Your sister had a strong motive, access to the cottage and the gun, and no alibi. Actually, with what you've just told me, it sounds like she admits she was near the cottage."

Cal's mouth fell open. "You're just like everyone else in this town. No one likes Monica. Sure, they all feel sorry for her, but it's easy to suspect someone you don't like."

Cal got in his truck, slammed the door and spun his tires on the way out.

Okay, Hannah thought to herself. Maybe that could have been handled better. Now she had a half finished cottage and no carpenter to finish the job. Maybe that was part of Monica's plan—to force Cal to quit to force Hannah to move away. Who knew what Monica's motive was?

Jack was walking back toward Hannah with Noah at his side. The poor kid, at least a half foot taller than his grandfather, was dragging his feet and his whole body slumped like he carried the weight of the world.

"You've got to hear Noah's story. Let's go inside." Jack looked around. "Where's Cal?"

"He left in a huff because I questioned something Monica said."

They walked inside. Cal had actually gotten quite a bit done already. The new stove, fridge, and counter were all installed. The sink was in place but no faucet, so the plumbing wasn't finished. Jack opened Hannah's fridge. Empty.

Hannah turned the knob for one of the stove burners and a red light came on. "The stove works. Anyone want some tea?" Jack wrinkled his nose and Noah shook his head. Hannah got out one cup for herself. "The only other option is water. She rummaged in a cardboard box that held a few items from the store. "Okay, the choices are trail mix," she held up her left hand, "or peanut butter crackers," she held up her right hand. "I didn't want to buy much food until Cal finished up in here."

Jack pointed to the trail mix. "Noah told me that Chase found them in the boat and told them to get out before he called Pam. Tasha went home and Noah hid out in your cabin again."

Hannah poured her tea and joined them at the table. "Noah. Why are you trying to hide from everyone? Are you in trouble?"

He sat with his head down and his hands hanging between his knees. “I don’t want to rat on Tasha, but I don’t think she cares about me anymore.”

With a soft voice, Hannah gently asked, “What haven’t you told anyone about Tasha? Was she at the cottage when Vern was killed?”

“I woke up when Mom left for work and I knew Tasha would be mad that I overslept.” Noah took a deep breath. “When I got here, I heard the gunshot and saw Tasha running away from the cottage. She ran in front of your cottage so she didn’t know I had come to meet her. That’s where she lost her gold chain. The one you found was hers, not mine.”

Hannah said, “I saw Tasha with her medallion after yours was found in the sand.”

“I gave her mine so her mother wouldn’t be suspicious.”

Hannah nodded. "Did you see anyone else?"

"Uh huh. I almost ran into Monica. She was coming down the path in her wheelchair when I turned to run away."

Hannah leaned toward Noah. "This is important. Was Monica on her way *to* the cottage or was she leaving it?"

Noah finally looked up. "She wasn't at the cottage. Tasha was."

Jack stood up. "Come on Noah. I'm taking you home. You need to tell this to your mother. She's half out of her mind, maybe completely out of her mind by now, with worry.

Noah walked out first and Hannah held Jack back for a minute. "I'm not sure if Cal will forgive me and come back to finish the job."

"What happened?"

"I more or less accused Monica of being the murderer. I should have listened to what you told me about the two of them. And now her story is the same as Noah's except Noah saw Tasha run the other way and Monica didn't say anything about that. Monica was pointing the blame at Noah."

Jack patted her shoulder. "Don't worry about it. Cal will cool down. Believe me, he'll be back. Meet me at the Clam Chowder Cook Off. Everyone's in for a big surprise."

With those words, Hannah noticed a twinkle in Jack's eyes. What was *that* about?

Chapter 21

Hannah took Nellie for a brisk walk on the beach before showering and changing. She wasn't even sure what a Clam Chowder Cook Off was, but with no place to make herself anything to eat, clam chowder sounded like the best option. Besides, maybe Ruby managed to uncover some more good information while she listened to the goings on at the Inn. Especially if Missy or Kelley had their mouths flapping.

She had her clean jeans on with her favorite burgundy fleece and hoped the cook off wasn't some sort of fancy affair or she'd stick out like a sore thumb. Oh well, nothing to do about that. She even dug out warm socks and sneakers, admitting to herself that it was too cold for flip flops.

The parking lot at the Paradise Inn was packed. Hannah parked her Volvo on the dirt at the end of the lot and hoped she wouldn't get towed, or worse, slide over the edge. Her passenger tires were dangerously close to the drop-off with nothing more than a row of granite blocks to keep her car where it was.

She looked around at all the people piling into the Inn and had a panic attack. She wasn't exactly fond of crowds but she took a deep breath and forced herself to head toward the front entryway. Jack was just arriving, carrying a small bag under his arm.

"Here. Take this." Jack stuffed his paper bag into Hannah's sling bag before she could protest or even ask what it was. "Don't worry, it's nothing that will get you arrested."

"Good to know. But now I *am* worried since I wasn't even thinking along those lines."

Jack whispered in Hannah's ear, "It's just a surprise for our favorite reporter. Sort of pay back from Caroline." He winked.

Before Hannah's brain had time to process that tidbit of information, the momentum of the crowd behind Hannah and Jack carried them inside like a school of fish. The lobby was decorated with greens, lights, and a beautiful Christmas tree. Tables were covered with every imaginable ocean trinket, from jewelry to paintings, pottery to handmade quilted items and baked goods that made Hannah's mouth water. This, obviously, was not the space for the Clam Chowder Cook Off.

Jack guided Hannah through the lobby to a big event room in the back. The seafood aroma met Hannah's nose and her stomach rumbled. Each cook had an area with a table for preparation and a portable electric burner. Meg waved them to her space.

The pot on her burner was erupting like a bubbling volcano.

"I thought you'd never get here," Meg hissed between tight lips. "I need all the moral support I can get with Kelley running the show this year. I can't believe the judges didn't disqualify her after Vern was murdered. It's a definite conflict of interest if you ask me. How can the judge be impartial to the person running the contest when she also has *her* clam chowder entered?"

Hannah looked around the room at the other tables. She counted twelve with Meg at one end and Kelley at the other side. Missy looked to be interviewing Kelley with her microphone moving back and forth between Missy's mouth and Kelley's mouth. The camera followed the microphone.

"Did Missy interview you yet?" Hannah asked Meg.

Meg snorted. "No. Kelley is getting all the attention."

Jack patted Meg's arm. "Don't worry about it. I have a plan. You just make sure your clam chowder is as good as ever and I guarantee you'll win again."

Ruby materialized next to Hannah. "I can't stay long but I wanted to tell you what Missy said to me."

Olivia pulled on Ruby's hand. "I'm bored," she announced, drawing out 'bored' until she ran out of air.

"Okay. Just a minute," Ruby answered before turning back to Hannah. "Missy predicted that Kelley would win the coveted clamshell bowl this year."

Hannah nodded her head in Kelley and Missy's direction. "It's pretty obvious that Missy is fawning all over Kelley, but Jack just assured Meg that she would win again this year."

Ruby looked around the room. "Is Cal coming?"

"I don't know. He left my cottage in a huff when I sort of implied I thought his sister might be Vern's murderer."

"Monica? Really?"

"That was before Noah showed up and told us that he saw Tasha running away from cottage number four right after the gunshot."

"Tasha? Kelley's daughter? I saw her here not too long ago. She was helping Kelley set up."

"I suppose Pam will be looking for her soon enough."

Olivia finally managed to get Ruby's attention and convince her to go back into the lobby where it was more interesting, at least to a five year old.

Meg handed Hannah a small bowl of her clam chowder to sample. "Does it need anything? I'm really nervous this year."

Hannah closed her eyes and slurped the chowder. "The only thing missing is more in my bowl," she kidded. "It's better than the chowder you made last night."

"Yeah, that was the practice run." Meg put the lid on her pot and wiped her hands on her apron. "What the devil is Jack doing now?"

Hannah looked to the other side of the room where Officer Pam Larson had pulled Kelley off to one side. Missy had her eyes on Kelley and no one was watching Kelley's pot of clam chowder as Jack lifted the lid and poured something into the pot.

Hannah patted her sling bag and realized the bag Jack asked her to carry was gone. As Jack hurried away, he knocked into the small table holding Kelley's bowls and spoons and everything crashed to the floor.

That got some attention.

"You clumsy old fool," Kelley scolded.

"Sorry Kelley. At least it wasn't your delicious clam chowder that tipped over." He bent down to help pick up the mess but Kelley pushed him away.

"You've done enough damage. Go harass someone else."

Jack moved back to Meg's table, barely containing his laughter. "Did you see her face? And that's just the beginning."

Hannah raised her eyebrows and looked at Meg. Meg shrugged.

Kelley raised her hands and asked the crowd for quiet. "It's time for the judge," she nodded toward Missy, "to sample the chowders. Everyone stand away from your pots. Once the judge has declared the winner, everyone else can have a taste."

Missy, wearing an ocean blue apron covered with clams, lifted the cover from Kelley's clam chowder first and ladled some into a bowl.

With great fanfare, Missy dipped her spoon into the chowder, blew on it, and swallowed. She smiled and took another big spoonful. Her eyes blinked several times before her mouth turned into a frown, she dropped the bowl, her hand went to her mouth, and she ran from the room.

Kelley's mouth fell open. Jack chuckled and the rest of the room erupted in laughter.

"I hope you got that on camera," Jack yelled to the cameraman who gave a thumbs up sign in response.

Kelley, her face red and contorted with rage, marched over to Jack, her finger wagging in his face. "It was you. You sabotaged my clam chowder."

Jack raised both eyebrows and held out his hands, palms up. "Me? I don't know what you could be talking about. I thought I saw Caroline drift through earlier. It must have been her."

Kelley put on her business smile and tried to calm everyone in the room. "I'm sure Missy will be right back and we'll be able to continue the judging. She was feeling a little under the weather all morning."

"Probably feeling under the weather in anticipation of tasting your clam chowder, Kelley," Jack said when there was finally a lull in the chatter. "I'd say she has a touch of food poisoning."

Kelley's nose flared and her jaw clenched but she had enough sense to keep quiet. She turned toward the door, smacking right into Officer Pam Larson.

"Oh. I'm glad to see you're back. I think someone sabotaged my clam chowder. Take a sample to your lab before anyone else gets sick."

Pam held onto Kelley's arm. "I'm here on some other business. I've just finished an interesting chat with your daughter, Tasha.

Apparently, she lied to me about her whereabouts the morning Vern was shot."

Kelley tried to pull her arm away but Pam held her firmly. "I don't know what you're talking about. We were both making chocolates at Simply Sweets Saturday morning. I arrived at six and Tasha arrived shortly after."

The room was dead silent. All eyes focused on Pam and Kelley.

Pam nodded. "Yes, that's what Tasha told me, but she also said you weren't feeling well and left about an hour later. Where did you go?"

Kelley's eyes darted around the room. "I went home to get some medicine for my stomach. I've had some indigestion lately," she added dramatically. "Then I had to make a stop at the Inn before I went back to the shop."

Tasha entered the room with Noah at her side. Jack leaned toward Hannah. "Do you know what's going on?"

Hannah shook her head. "No, but I have a feeling it's not going to end well for someone."

"Tasha! Tell Officer Larson that I came back to help you finish up with the chocolates. It's such a busy time of year for Simply Sweets and Paradise Inn. I don't have good help and, unfortunately, I can't be in two places at once. I have to run between the two businesses constantly. Tell her, Tasha."

Tasha's arms were clenched tight across her chest. Her eyes swam with tears. "No, Mom. I can't keep lying for you, especially not when you tried to ruin Noah's life by making everyone believe he did something wrong. The only thing he's done is be my best friend, especially when I couldn't count on *you*. You almost had me believing your lies until you tried to blame him for robbing the safe. I saw *you* take that money out."

Tears streamed down Tasha's cheeks. Noah put his arm around her shoulders and supported her sagging body.

"Lies! It's all lies," Kelley shouted, as if it was more believable at a louder decibel. "Don't believe a word she's saying. Tasha was at the cottage when Vern was shot. I saw her." With that statement, Kelley's hand went to cover her mouth.

"That's right, Mom, I *was* at the cottage. You saw me right after you shot your husband in the chest. *You* saw me run away—but I saw *you* kill Vern."

Chapter 22

Officer Pam Larson escorted Kelley from the Clam Chowder Cook Off room. Everyone started talking at once.

Jack hugged his grandson, leading him and Tasha to the side of the room next to Meg's clam chowder table. Hannah ladled clam chowder into bowls for everyone standing nearby, assuming the competition was done for the day.

One voice asking for a bowl made the corners of Hannah's lips curve into a smile. She handed chowder to Cal. "You missed all the excitement."

"I watched Kelley try to maintain her dignity as she was stuffed into the back of the police cruiser. What happened?"

Hannah filled Cal in on the details as they enjoyed Meg's delicious clam chowder. "There is one thing that I haven't figured out yet." She hesitated. "Don't take this the wrong way, but why was Monica sneaking through the path, spying on the cottages?"

Cal shrugged. "Monica told me she was obsessed with spying on Vern after the accident. She could never forgive him. Not because of how it changed her life, but because I dropped out of med school to help her. When she saw his car parked by that path to your cottages, she made regular trips with her new wheelchair to find out what he was up to. I hope she can finally put it all behind her, especially since I think I've convinced her that I'm happy being a carpenter."

Jack, with a wide grin across his face, set his empty bowl of chowder on Meg's table. "Kelley was darn close to getting away with murder. Good thing Caroline came back to help get the truth out!"

Ruby and Olivia appeared next to Hannah. "I just got a call from Missy's boss. Apparently they fired her for believing all that malarkey about Caroline being the murderer. It hurt the credibility of the station. He said he'd be in touch when they replace Missy." Ruby hugged Hannah. "Can you believe it? If he offers me a job, we'll be able to stay here in Hooks Harbor with you."

Cal grinned. "I better get another cottage all fixed up for you and Olivia, or will you be sharing cottage number one with Hannah?"

Hannah rolled her eyes in Cal's direction.

"No." Ruby stepped back. "I'll find something in town, close to the elementary school and the shops. Olivia can visit the beach but I think we need a bit of space between us." Ruby put her hand on Hannah's arm, her eyes filled with concern. "You're okay with that, aren't you?"

Hannah picked up Olivia. "Your plan sounds perfect."

Meg looked at her table piled with empty bowls of clam chowder. "No clamshell bowl to add to Caroline's collection, but it was worth it to see Missy's green face as she ran for the bathroom."

Hannah scraped every last bit of clam chowder from her bowl. "As far as I'm concerned, Great Aunt Caroline's clam chowder will always be the best in Hooks Harbor!"

The End

A Note from Lyndsey

Thank you for reading my cozy mystery, *Gunpowder Chowder*.

Sign up for my newsletter to find out about my latest releases which are always offered at a discount price to my Cozy Mystery Club:

http://lyndseycolebooks.com/

ABOUT THE AUTHOR

Lyndsey Cole lives in New England in a small rural town with her husband, dogs, cats and chickens. She has plenty of space to grow lots of beautiful perennials. Sitting in the garden with the scent of lilac, peonies, lily of the valley or whatever is in bloom, stimulates her imagination about mysteries and romance.

ONE LAST THING . . .

If you enjoyed this installment of The Hannah Holiday Cozy Mystery Series, be sure to join my FREE COZY MYSTERY BOOK CLUB! Be in the know for new releases, promotions, sales, and the possibility to receive advanced reader copies. Join the club here—
http://LyndseyColeBooks.com

OTHER BOOKS BY LYNDSEY COLE

The Black Cat Café Series

BlueBuried Muffins

Annie Fisher is scared. She's scared of the mess her boyfriend, Max Parker, is in the middle of and she has to get out of his house. She puts a whole state between them and drives like a madwoman from Cooper, NY to her hometown of Catfish Cove, NH where she hopes she'll be safe.

She decides to start a new life, a life she ran away from two years ago but is finding herself missing as soon as she gets home. Annie immediately has a place to live, a job at her Aunt Leona's new café—Black Cat Café—and plenty of boyfriend prospects. Unfortunately, she also has plenty of bad things follow her.

Like Max Parker. Only the next time she sees him he's dead. Suddenly everyone she runs into turns into a potential suspect. There are ghosts from her past and new neighbors that make her hair stand on end.

And right in the middle of everything is Annie with Max's last warning to her—Don't trust anyone. Will those words prove to keep her safe or put too much distance between Annie and those trying to help her?

StrawBuried in Chocolate

Annie Fisher wakes up on Friday the thirteenth, but she reminds herself she's not superstitious. The Black Cat Café is loaded up with special Valentine's Day goodies, the most popular being Annie's chocolate covered strawberries. She is so looking forward to a romantic weekend with current flame, landlord and neighbor, Jason Hunter.

But when her Aunt Leona finds a body in Jason's house, all plans for that romantic weekend are scrapped. All Annie, Leona, Mia and Jason can think about is who killed Lacy McGuire and why.

With more and more clues pointing toward Leona as the killer, they need to work fast to figure out who the real killer is before Leona ends up in jail for good. To complicate matters for Annie, information surfaces about her birth parents, a mystery she's been working on for the past few years. She thinks she wants to find the answers, but will it destroy her world?

Now, Annie must struggle to save her aunt, but as she questions neighbors and relatives, will she put herself in danger with the real killer? Will she save her aunt but get herself killed in the process?

BlackBuried Pie

The Fourth of July weekend promises lots of excitement for the cozy town of Catfish Cove. A dog parade, bonfire, barbecue and fireworks are sure to bring in the crowds and give a boost to all businesses, including the Black Cat Café.

To prepare for the onslaught of customers, Annie Fisher has to keep their supply up of blackberries from Hayworth Fruit Farms for everyone's favorite, blackberry pie. But when she finds the berry farmer unconscious in his field, her mind immediately goes to the worst possible scenario. To make matters worse, the farmer's neighbor turns up dead and anonymous messages drag Annie into the mystery when all she wants to do is spend time with her handsome boyfriend.

With clues pointing in every direction, Annie needs to figure out who's lying and who she can trust before she ends up as the next victim in the killer's web of deceit.

Very Buried Cheesecake

This should be an exciting time for Annie with the opening of her new art gallery, but she's stressed and distracted preparing for her first photography opening. With her friend Martha and her new employee, Camilla, working to get the gallery set up, everything seems to be on track.

But when Annie stumbles on a body floating at the edge of Heron Lake, her worst fears are realized. Memories of her previous photography exhibit and the ensuing murder investigation come back to haunt her.

To make matters worse, the new detective in town points her finger at Annie right from their first meeting at the crime scene. Is this an ominous sign of what's in store for Annie? With mysterious money disappearing and stolen jewelry showing up from thin air, a pre wedding dinner cruise and Martha's on again/off again wedding, all is not what it seems.

Now Annie struggles to avoid being sucked into the mayhem. Will she be able to put her fears aside and figure out how to stay ahead of the killer?

RaspBuried Torte

When renovations on an old house in Catfish Cove take a turn for the worse, Annie finds herself at odds with the new detective in town. Again. Not only did Annie find the body, but Detective Christy Crank seems to have a chip on her shoulder that she takes out on Annie.

Rumors of hidden fortunes in the walls of the old house bring out treasure hunters in droves. Could one of them have killed to secure their own fortune? And if so, who was it?

As Annie digs deeper to clear the name of her friend, and Cranky's top suspect, Danny Davis, she uncovers lies about alibis that only add more suspects to her list. Dreams of wealth make plenty of people look guilty, but who is the real murderer?

Annie knows she has to figure it out with the help of her friends before Danny takes the fall for something he didn't do. Will she make it in time before the killer comes back to cover their tracks?

PoisonBuried Punch

Halloween—parties, costumes, decorations, pranks and . . . murder? Annie Fisher and her friends at the Black Cat Café are right in on all the town's Halloween excitement with everyone competing for the best couples costume award.

But when a man turns up dead, a real-life Halloween murder comes to Catfish Cove. With Annie's friend as the main suspect, she finds herself caught up in the whirlwind of sorting through stories, alibis, and new suspects. When loyalties change and true identities are revealed, Annie isn't sure what is true or who is lying.

With each new twist and turn, Annie tries to stay one step ahead of the killer so she can clear her friend's name and stay safe herself. As time ticks away and she gets closer and closer to the truth, she begins to question her own mortality. Who can she believe? And more importantly, who can she trust with her life?

The Lily Bloom Series

Begonias Mean Beware

Misty Valley has a new flower shop in town, and as soon as Lily Bloom hangs the open sign, she lands the biggest wedding in town. Plus, the handsome new guy moves in right next door to Lily. She's well on her way to a successful and exciting season.

But when the groom is found dead in her kitchen just days before he's supposed to be walking down the aisle, Lily has to arrange the trail of flowers to try to solve the mystery. With the help of her scooter-riding, pot-smoking mother, Iris, her sister, Daisy, and her dog, Rosie, Lily races from one disaster to another, all the while keeping herself out of the killer's sight.

Will she solve the cascade of events in time or get caught by the criminals running illegal gambling and selling drugs in Misty Valley? Will romance blossom between Lily and her new neighbor?

Queen of Poison

Business at Lily's Beautiful Blooms Flower Shop is growing like weeds after a rainstorm. She's been asked to do the main flower arrangement for the Arts in Bloom opening at the Misty Valley Museum. Everything seems to be coming up rosy and she's even falling head over heels for the man of her dreams, Ryan Steele, her neighbor and the police chief of Misty Valley.

Until she sees a sleek red convertible drive into his driveway. And an even sleeker red head climbs out of the car. She thought that was all she had to deal with until the founder of the museum drops dead in her arms and another body has all fingers pointing toward Lily.

With help from her mom, Iris, her sister, Daisy and their friends Marigold and Tamara, Lily tries to arrange the clues to point to the real killer. Can she sort it out in time before a third body—maybe hers—ends up in the morgue? Can she get her romance growing again with the handsome police chief of Misty Valley? Or will she be left to sort through the clues alone?

Roses are Dead

Business is popping for Lily as wedding season is in full swing. The brides are all over the place from easy-to-please to last-minute-panics. But one in particular stands out—a leggy brunette who is looking for plenty of red roses for her wedding to Police Chief Ryan Steele.

Lily is beside herself with betrayal that Ryan would lead her on like that, all the while engaged to this beauty. It's almost too much to take until the bride is found dead, surrounded by none other than the very roses she'd been admiring.

Lily shoots to the top of the suspect list, a place she's been all too often lately. And as she starts to uncover more about the woman's past, she's thrown into another game of cat and mouse. Only she's not sure if she's the cat or the mouse. Will she be able to follow the clues to the real killer in time? Or is everyone connected to Ryan Steele in danger and Lily could be next?

Drowning in Dahlias

The business is heating up at Beautiful Blooms and Lily's flower arrangements can be found all over Misty Valley at any type of event. And to add to the chaos, she's lost the full time help of her sister, Daisy, who has started a specialty cake making business on the side. Together, they make the perfect team, especially when wealthy estate owner, Walter Nash, enlists both of them to cater and decorate for the 55th birthday party for his wife.

But when they show up with their deliveries and find the love of his life, Harriet Nash, dead on the floor, the dynamic duo is suddenly threatened. With a house full of family and friends to celebrate her birthday, there are too many suspects to keep straight.

Lily's biggest challenge now is to find the killer before the killer finds her. But without a murder weapon at the crime scene, the questions continue to pile up without any answers. Who would have wanted Harriet dead the most? She had plenty of money, but would someone have been so greedy? As Lily and Daisy get closer to solving the murder, things take a turn for the worse with a threat on Lily's life.

Hidden by the Hydrangeas

Lily Bloom can't seem to keep her thoughts away from marriage. Maybe it's just because her mom tied the knot with her childhood sweetheart Walter Nash, but it's gotten Lily thinking about her own relationship with Ryan Steele and if it's going anywhere.

But those thoughts are quickly replaced with who is carrying a dead body, and who that dead body might be. The only thing Lily knows is that she's been spotted by the killer so she has to hope this mystery is solved before she's the next one in a body bag.

When Walter's best friend turns up as the likeliest suspect, Lily's mom is beside herself with worry and convinces Lily that she's the best person to solve this case. But suspects keep piling up with not quite enough evidence to prove anything. Will Lily be able to put all the pieces together before the killer sniffs out her trail?

Christmas Tree Catastrophe

Lily Bloom couldn't be more excited for Christmas Eve when she will say "I do" to the man she loves. She just has the library opening to get through and then all the town's focus will be on her.

But things start going wrong almost from the very first moment she's getting setup for the library's event. Not only is there plenty of disagreement among those helping, but one of the co-chairs who is in charge of the whole event winds up dead the day before the ceremony.

With everyone who was helping setup under a microscope, Lily is in a race against time to be able to get married. When one of her best friends winds up in jail for the murder Lily knows she didn't commit, the pressure's on to find the real murderer.

Will Lily be able to prove her friend's innocence? Or will she find herself in even more trouble and face a wedding in a jail cell or the hospital? Or worse—will there be no wedding at all because the bride is the new target?

CPSIA information can be obtained at www.ICGtesting.com
Printed in the USA
BVOW08s2222151215

430395BV00002B/46/P